James Francis Rosslyn

Sonnets and Poems

Dedicated to the Queen

James Francis Rosslyn

Sonnets and Poems
Dedicated to the Queen

ISBN/EAN: 9783744711944

Printed in Europe, USA, Canada, Australia, Japan

Cover: Foto ©Andreas Hilbeck / pixelio.de

More available books at **www.hansebooks.com**

SONNETS AND POEMS

BY THE

EARL OF ROSSLYN

DEDICATED TO THE QUEEN

London

REMINGTON & CO.

HENRIETTA STREET, COVENT GARDEN

1889

Deal with us gently, ye who read!
  Our largest hope is unfulfilled—
The promise still outruns the deed—
  The tower, but not the spire, we build.

Our whitest pearl we never find;
  Our ripest fruit we never reach;
The flowering moments of the mind
  Drop half their petals in our speech.

OLIVER WENDELL HOLMES.

.

.   .   .   .   .

.   .   .   .   .

.   .   .   .   .

And thus, as in memory's bark we shall glide,
  To visit the scenes of our boyhood anew,
Though oft we may see, looking down on the tide,
  The wreck of full many a hope shining through;
Yet still, as in fancy we point to the flowers
  That once made a garden of all the gay shore,
Deceiv'd for a moment, we'll think them still ours,
  And breathe the fresh air of life's morning once more.

MOORE'S *Irish Melodies.*

TO

VICTORIA, REGINA ET IMPERATRIX

If I should write and praise the Sun's rich ray,
And say it lights up all the gloomy ground,
And warms the heart and life of all around,
And makes dull labour into cheerful play ;
Turns dark to bright, grave thought supplants by gay,
Where nothing flourishes, bids all abound,
And with an equal warmth for all is found,
I should but laud God's gift of every day.
So must I sing, as rivalling the Sun
In wide-extended Empire, and in good
That reaches all, and comforts all, Thy Fame
Who rulest half the Globe ; and, thus begun,
I could not end—such vast and grateful food
Thy praise supplies !—such love Thy honoured Name !

ROSSLYN.

November 1889.

INTRODUCTION

LORD ROSSLYN, being still an invalid, has not been able to give this volume the final revision which he would have so much desired. He has, however, read through the proofsheets as the book was going to press. Many of the poems have already appeared in print, either in periodicals or in books for private circulation. On the other hand, some of them are quite new, and the book may be considered a more or less complete collection of LORD ROSSLYN'S poetical works. The spirit in which he now gives it to the Public is embodied by himself in the following pathetic note.—

' When, at the instigation of my friends, I ventured to publish a modest volume of sonnets, the compilation of which had extended over nearly three decades, I felt how inadequate the result was to the time it had occupied, and I trembled lest *the parturition of the mountain should in my case, as in so many others, be an accomplished fact. Whether from the kindness of the critics, or the modest nature of the motto which I selected and have retained in the present volume, or the indulgence of my friends, I know not; but true it is that I had to encounter only a too favourable reception, and the whole edition was speedily exhausted. I have since refrained from again tempting the perilous path; but now a lingering and dangerous illness, but half surmounted, warns me that I have only a short space left in which to throw myself upon the consideration of the public. I avail myself of it, not indeed as I could once have done, but yet gratefully and gladly, and yield to those whose better judgment has always been my guiding star, and who have, in this case, urged me to publish some poems as well as my favourite sonnets. Among these " The Jubilee Lyric," printed by the gracious command of Her Majesty, and some translations from Greek, French, Russian, and Italian authors, trifling in themselves, will be found. They are all unworthy of serious consideration; but, as they have rendered many hours of my past life happier and better, I trust they will be accepted as they are meant, to pass an idle moment, and they will assuredly in no instance call a blush to the cheek of either the maiden or the youth who may peruse them. Should it please God to restore me to health,*

I may, I trust, be excused for hoping that the favour with which these verses may be received will be an inducement to write more. '*ROSSLYN.*'

The Editor's share in this volume has mainly been the categorical arrangement of the pieces; and he anxiously hopes that this task, a labour of love, has been fulfilled in a manner that the admirers of the Poet will approve.

By gracious permission, this volume is dedicated to Her Majesty the Queen.

W. EARL HODGSON.

LONDON: November 1889.

CONTENTS

---·◦·---

TO MY WIFE

AFTER PETRARCH

IN MEMORIAM

TYROLEAN SONNETS

AND OTHER SONNETS OF TRAVEL

CALVARY

AND OTHER SONNETS OF MEDITATION

SONNETS IN OTHER THAN ITALIAN FORM

CONTENTS

STANZAS FOR MUSIC

INSOMNIA

AND OTHER MISCELLANEOUS POEMS

CONTENTS

TO MY WIFE

B

TO MY WIFE

I

LIGHT of my life, dear Wife, I write to thee;

    Do not like captious critic judge my lines,

For my whole heart, like ivy, intertwines

The words so old, yet ever new to me!

In all thy sufferings I must bear my part,

As in thy joys I joy to have my share;

And if, to-night, God gives thee more to bear,

I too will bear it, with a willing heart.

Life is made up of suffering and delight—

Suffering, short-lived; delight, thank God, how long!—

And ere the sunrise of to-morrow's morn

Thou wilt forget the anguish of to-night;

And through long years thou wilt recall my song,

And, smiling, cry, 'No rose without a thorn.'

II

WHEN all my thoughts are turned to thee alone,

How can I sleep, except I dream of thee?

How can I, waking, join in gaiety,

When half my smiles for thee are woe-begone?

Thou art my Sun! and if my Sun has shone,

I glory like a lizard, basking free

In the full noon-tide of my revelry,

Or like a welcome courtier near the throne.

But darker dreams will force their dreadful way

Through the long watch of night, and sunny hours

Sometimes will yield to vapours from the East.

Shine, then, sweet Wife, like hawthorn buds in May

With opening promise! and, Celestial powers,

Send us blest fruit from love's abundant feast!

III

O FEAR ! O Hope ! sisters, alas ! in blood,
　　And yet of alien races !　Why does Fate
Blend all my life with yours ?　I wait and wait
In Hope and Fear each night—an anxious mood !
Love ! many cruel words hast thou withstood,
But thou must bear this blame ; I learn too late
Thou drivest Sleep through the fair ivory gate,
And Fear and Hope spring from thy varied brood ;
Yet, in my Hope, Fear holds me somewhat right,
Lest I grow over-fond, and in my Fear
Hope cheers me onward, lest I all despair ;
And in both Hope and Fear love clasps me tight,
And keeps me ever watchful o'er my Dear,
Whose joys and sorrows are my fondest care !

IV

WHOM can I love but thee? Is not my heart,

So full of love, wholly and solely thine?

And if true love—of earth the one divine,

Unchanging, holy thing—thou dost impart,

It were strange barter in an unfair mart,

Did I not give—nay, lay upon the shrine

I best can worship at, that poor thing—mine.

On life's rough ocean take it for thy chart!

And now, when Nature's tribute, Love's harsh toll,

Weighs heavily on thy spirit, learn Love's lore

From fondest volume, certified and sure.

Emblazoned on imperishable scroll,

Our love shall shine, Belovèd, more and more,

And deathless through all ages shall endure!

V

THE Spring, long since, has shaded her blue eyes
  With the thick verdure of the Summer leaves;

And now the heart o'er parting Summer grieves,

Loath to greet Autumn and her cloudy skies.

Yet, in despite of sorrow, Autumn comes

Rich with her golden gifts, and bounteous store

She brings to gladden many a cottage door,

And send the gleaners happy to their homes.

Too soon will Autumn, shivering, shrink away,

And leafless winter, herald of Christ's birth,

Bring other hopes, and whisper holier joy.

Thus every season has its happy day;

God gives to each its own allotted mirth:

Most blest to thee the one that brings thy Boy.

VI

SLEEP soundly, Sweetheart, though the winds blow high
  And snow-wreaths crown the buds of early spring;
Like a true mate, at resting-time I sing
A tender carol for thy lullaby.
Dread nothing, Dearest, when thy love is nigh,
And nestle close beneath the downy wing
Of slumber; spite of tempests murmuring,
Thy God will guard thee with a Father's eye.
Blest in thy faith, thy children, and thy love,
Raise, ere thou sleep'st, to God thy grateful heart,
Whose mercy keeps thee both by night and day;
Lift thy dear voice in praise and prayer above,
So shalt thou prosper in that better part
He promises to all who watch and pray.

I LECTURE? Sweet! when thou art near, thy eyes
  Discourse unanswerably to my heart;
And all my reason, all my nobler part,
Yields to thy lecture's tender sympathies.
As the loud notes are hushed in symphonies,
And bend their music to consummate art,
Lulled by a skill no untrained hands impart,
So sinks my soul in gratified surprise.
Surprise ! nay, why surprise? for Love must rule
In every moment of my happiest hours,
In every motion of my too-blest life,
And whip me back, a dullard, to that school
Where learning ever laughs; where, crowned with flowers,
My sternest master is my darling Wife.

VIII

YOU bid me write a sonnet to the year,
    Whose dying moments tremble in the grasp
Of Time's relentless hand, whose final gasp—
Feeble and faint—comes nearer, and more near.
Dearest, thy loving hand dries every tear;
And every moment, fleeting but too fast,
Speaking so solemnly of the changeless past,
But tells me truly that you grow more dear.
The gentle guidance of a Heavenly grace,
Thy guileless sympathy for others' woe,
Sustain thee in thy trials from above,
Lend a new charm to thy endearing face;
And if thou needest comfort from below,
Oh, seek it always in thy husband's love!

December 31, 1868.

IX

OH, blame me not because my verse is rare!

Deem not my heart is idle as my song!

Thou know'st to thee such melodies belong,

As my poor pen can haltingly prepare;

But my full heart of no such blame takes share,

And to blame that would do it grievous wrong,

For still its stream flows passionate and strong,

And pays no tribute but to thee, my Fair!

If, then, I sing not, 'tis because, too full,

The river of my heart o'erleaps its banks,

And to one ocean, thine, pours out its tide;

And mocking spirits might proclaim me dull,

And even thou wouldst give me meagre thanks,

If, while I praised thee, others should deride.

X

DOST thou regret the seeming hard decrees
        Of Providence, sweet Wife, that keep thee far
From thy dear children?   Yonder glittering star
Is far removed from us, yet still it sees
With loving light each night upon thy knees
Thy suppliant form pray God no ill may mar
Thy darlings, or no cruel chance debar
That blissful meeting when His will shall please.
Regret them not: that star is like thy heart,
Distant, yet ever present, pure and bright,
And, though so very far, is ever near.
Soon shall all sickness pass, and then thy part
Of hopeful waiting for the promised light
Will be rewarded without stint or fear.

XI

MORN after morn I tremble at each sound,
  That breaks my loved one's short uneasy sleep;
Fever and pain their constant vigil keep,
And I, poor sentinel, pace my dreary round.
Ah me! what sounds of horror do abound
In this great city ere the sunbeams peep
From out their cloudy coverlet! Yon Steep,
With battlemented castle grimly crowned,
Is first, with bugle-blare, the day to greet;
And then belated brawlers stagger home,
And heavy wains, high-laden with the store
Of country produce, grind along the street;
And engines, savage whistling, slowly come,
And cruel hammers beat the neighbouring floor.

EDINBURGH : 1876.

XII

(To be read with No. XI.)

H OW quakes my heart at each! my nerves strung tight,
 Wrestling with all these fiends that murder sleep,
Sink in untuned vibration; and I weep
From very weakness; till at last the light
Dawns fuller, rosier, on my wearied sight.·
And once again the tram-cars jingling creep,
And jostling cabs run rattling up the steep,
And a stray sunbeam makes the world more bright.
Sleep on, in spite of all, for love has won
The victory for thee; and soon, sweet Wife,
Thou shalt forget thy sorrow and thy pain,
And, in returning health (now scarce begun),
Shalt find new hopes to animate thy life,
And e'en from suffering make a lasting gain.

EDINBURGH: *October* 8, 1876.

XIII

MY VALENTINE

ONCE more I write to thee.   Ten changeful years
　　Have brought maturer love and not less true :
Our mid-day sun shines proudly, though the hue
He sheds is deeper than the morning wears,
And gold and violet, not rose-tint, appears.
Dearest ! nor time nor care can make us rue,
If in life's eventide our heaven of blue
No darker shade than God's own sunset bears !
Thou hast been brave in suffering; and in joy
No heart more joyous; thou hast shared with me
A Decade of life's trials—not severe,
But still life's trials: gold without alloy
Serves scanty purpose: mayst thou ever be
Blest in that Love which casteth out all Fear.

February 14, 1876.

XIV

'TOUT VIENT À POINT À QUI SAIT ATTENDRE'

IF to good waiters all things good arrive—

As speaks the ancient proverb in my text—

Then may I call thee 'good,' and though perplext

As stranger Bee within an unknown hive,

Yet welcome as the day; oh, mayst thou thrive

In virtue and in wisdom! rarely vext

By the world's troubles, and the cares annext

By cruel Fate to everything alive!

Dear 'Boy'—sweet little word to mother's ears

Whose nursery teems with girls!—sweet sound to me

Whose lineage languished, last of an old race

Which her love lovingly renewed, whose fears

Are now a saucy jest between us three,

Though when I smile she hides her joyous face.

XV

OUR TWELFTH WEDDING-DAY

HOW strangely swift advancing years roll by,
  Laden with joy's and sorrow's mingled load,

Down the dark path of life's uneven road,

Whose milestones' only mark is Memory!

Twelve years have passed, Sweetheart, since thou and I

Joined hand to hand and vowed our vows to God

And to each other, and as one abode;

And thus may we abide until we die!

By sickness sorely saddened and oppressed,

Yet urged by love that knows no dull decline,

Thou hast kept Tryst—twelve touching years do prove

Thou on thy husband's constant heart canst rest;

Thy arms with his once more canst intertwine,

And laugh at Time that only adds to love.

November 8, 1878.

OTHER DOMESTIC OR SOCIAL

SONNETS

TO MILLIE,

WITH aching heart just seventeen years ago

    I wrote of thee, my first-born ; thou wert sent

To bid the old tree show new increment

And promise in the midst of bitter woe :—

Thy Mother in death's grasp well-nigh laid low,

My sister, of our race the ornament,

Struck sudden lifeless ; ' Only Millicent,

Poor Babe,' I cried, 'remaineth to me now ! '

My cry reached Heaven ! Dear Mother lives

To bless both thee and me ; thy brothers smile,

And grasp at manhood ere their time be come ;

Grace to thy sisters all her tribute gives ;

I see thee loving and beloved, the while

Thy Husband bears thee to another home.

October 12, 1884.

LOYAL JE SERAI DURANT MA VIE

The old French motto was shortened by Stafford to 'Loyal je serai,' in a troth ring which he gave Millie; the meaning evidently being that his loyalty would endure beyond life itself—hence the Sonnet.

WHY should Life's span my Loyalty confine?

Or bind my Duty with so slight a chain?

Though we be parted we shall meet again;

And wilt thou less in Heaven's pure home be mine?

Is earthly Love more sure than Love divine?

Nay, dearest, if my weeping eyes remain

To dew thy grave and suffer tenderest pain,

I still would be thine only—only thine!

But if that Spirit unto whom we pray

First take me, lonely in that blissful throng,

Apart from thee, there will I wait and wait

And feed upon thy coming day by day

For ever Loyal, and in patience strong,

Till thou shalt enter the Eternal Gate.

August 17, 1884.

HOME

TO BLANCHIE A FEW DAYS BEFORE HER MARRIAGE

SWEET word that spans all space, that knows no bound,

 Yet dwells in narrowest compass; welcome word!

Dear type of Peace—yet sheltered by the sword:

Mid Saxon-speaking races only found.

Our earliest recollections all abound

With little notes of thee; our years are stored

With memories of thee; each spot adored

By youth, in age becometh holy ground.

Thou clingest in the handgrip of the Sire;

Thou meltest in the Mother's tender kiss;

The wanderer longs to reach thee—Guiding Star

Of all his thoughts: like Israel's Pillared Fire,

By night thou leadest him through childhood's bliss,

To that loved home he pictures from afar.

August 26, 1886.

TO DAISY

CHILD of my love, though yet not mine in blood,
    How farest thou now? beaming with blue-eyed mirth
And rose-hued health? What corner of the earth
Fills thy young head? That carnage-stricken flood
Where the slow Othman with persistent mood
Beats back the lying Russ? Doth pale-eyed dearth,
That haunts the Madrassee's penurious hearth,
  Beg for thy pity—for his daily food?
Or, Darling, doth the Jasmine climb too high?
Or red-roan Ellie seek her wonted crust?
Or loud-voiced Spangle call his faithful dame?
Do these attract thee? or, although less nigh,
Are thy thoughts given in unreservèd trust
To me, thy Father in all else save name?

TO HARRY

I T is no blame, my Boy, to thee nor me,
  If I should be severe or seem so now;
For love exacts perfection, asks not how,
But sternly claims the rightful deed should be.
E'en so, my love demands all things from thee,
That should beseem the seeds that in thee grow,
And plant completeness on thy smooth young brow;
The well-trained sapling makes the fairest tree.
Be guided, then, by thy fond Father's word:
Make honest men thy friends, thy watchword Truth;
Be generous as thou mayest; hating strife,
Protect the weak; and if thou draw'st the sword,
Ne'er sheathe it till victorious.   Make thy youth
The pure first chapter of thy Book of Life.

January 29, 1881.

BEDTIME

'TIS bedtime; say your hymn, and bid 'Good-night;
    God bless Mamma, Papa, and dear ones all;'
Your half-shut eyes beneath your eyelids fall,
Another minute you will shut them quite.
Yes, I will carry you, put out the light,
And tuck you up, although you are so tall!
What will you give me, Sleepy one, and call
My wages, if I settle you all right?
I laid her golden curls upon my arm,
I drew her little feet within my hand,
Her rosy palms were joined in trustful bliss,
Her heart next mine beat gently, soft and warm
She nestled to me, and, by Love's command,
Paid me my precious wages—'Baby's Kiss.'

October 30, 1882.

OLD LETTERS

I T seems but yesterday she died ; but years
   Have passed since then : the wondrous change of time
Makes great things little, little things sublime,
And sanctifies the dew of daily tears.
She died, as all must die ; no trace appears
In History's page, nor save in my poor rhyme,
Of her, whose life was love, whose lovely prime
Passed sadly where no sorrows are, nor fears.
It seems but yesterday ; to-day I read
A few short letters in her own dear hand,
And doubted if 'twere true.   Their tender grace
Seems radiant with her life !   Oh ! can the Dead
Thus in their letters live ?   I tied the band,
And kissed her name as though I kissed her face.

MEMORY

I STILL keep open Memory's chamber: still
    Drink from the fount of Youth's perennial stream.
It may be in old age an idle dream
Of those dear children; but beyond my will
They come again, and dead affections thrill
My pulseless heart, for now once more they seem
To be alive, and wayward fancies teem
In my fond brain, and all my senses fill.
Come, Alice, leave your books; 'tis I who call;
Bind up your hair, and teasing—did you say
Kissing—that kitten?   Evey, come with me;
Mary, grave darling, take my hand; yes, all!
I have three hands to-day!   A Holiday.
A Holiday, Papa?   Woe's me! 'tis Memory!

AT PLAY

A N April day! The cruel wind had fled,
　　And from the West a gentle zephyr came;
The speckled Thrush sang joyously, and tame
The cooing Wood Doves made their nuptial bed.
The cricket ground, new mown, our youngsters led
To tempt the flying ball—a glorious game
Where English boys may proudly keep the name
Of English sport from growing dull and dead.
The great Park Roller made an eminence—
Albeit cold as iron is, and brown
With recent labour—and I saw thereon,
Seated like any Queen, to view from thence
The pastime, my small daughter; but my frown,
A rude republican, disturbed her throne.

AMONG MY BOOKS

ALONE, 'midst living works of mighty dead,
　　Poets and scholars versed in history's lore,
With thoughts that reached beyond them and before,
I dream, and leave their glorious works unread;
Their greatness numbs me both in heart and head.
I cannot weep with Petrarch, and still more
I fail when I would delve the depths of yore,
And learn old Truths of modern lies instead;
The shelves frown on me blackly, with a life
That ne'er can die, and, helpless to begin,
I can but own my weakness, and deplore
This waste, this barren brain, ah! once so rife
With hope and fancy.　Pardon all my sin,
Great Ghosts that wander on the Eternal Shore.

December 24, 1876.

WORK AND REST

GIVE my brain work! the enthusiast wildly cries;
  Give my brain rest! the weary toiler prays.
Rest pains; work pains: both follow different ways,
Yet each demands relief and sympathies.
Give each their prayer! the toiler, resting, dies;
The enthusiast, losing strength and hope, decays;
Though both, illumined by the mind's bright rays,
Love the dear pain, and hug their agonies.
Thus pain for work devised, completed not,
And pain for overwork, are brethren twain;
Dissimilar, yet alike: poor strugglers, rest;
The longing heart, though failing, makes no blot;
And energetic labour should not pain;
But both united must indeed be blest!

1860.

BRAIN v. MUSCLE

THERE is no labour like to idleness,

    When the heart's vigour must restrainèd be

And the keen yearnings yield to apathy;

This prisoning of the mind is sore distress,

And is a curse, where toil itself would bless,

And make a healthy spirit fair and free

Beneath Heaven's wide and welcome canopy,

That covers workers with a great caress.

True, to brain-strugglers, whose enforcèd rest

Is misery; less true to sinewy slaves

Who sweat, and faint, and long for mere repose.

Could we but join their tasks, the sum were best,

And aged men would scoff at early graves,

And happy peasants soon forget their woes.

May 29, 1885.

MIDNIGHT, 1872-3

FLY not, old year, too swiftly; say 'Good-bye,'

　　Let us part friends, shake hands before you go;

Time tolls out 'Yes,' when neither can say 'No,'

And these harsh partings dim the brightest eye.

It is not that we fear the end more nigh,

For the great end brings joy instead of woe,

When we may join the loved ones long laid low,

And change for angel-smile our earthly sigh;

But that, Old Friend, we know not what may come,

Of sorrow and regret, when thy young Heir

Has set thy crown upon his brow.　Farewell!

Alas! farewell for ever!　Here at home

Grateful I own thy blessings and thy care,

And listen sadly to thy funeral knell.

IN THE CLUB-ROOM

ONCE more, by God's good grace, I watch the time

    Draw slowly on to sound the last dread knell

Of the old Year; and like the funeral bell,

Ring out the dirge of death with muffled chime.

In every land, in every varied clime,

Hearts at this time have something new to tell

Both of the past and future, ill or well,

And often laughter checks the sad sublime.

Extremes meet in the busy club-room—here

The oldest fogey and the youngest boy

Jostle in word and thought; yet minutes fly,

And with still step creeps in the infant Year;

Then old and young shake hands.　May months of joy

Be thine, young Year!　Good-bye, old Year, good-bye!

December 31, 1876, 11.40 P.M.

OLD FRIENDS

IF there should be in other climes than these,

    When I am dead, a thought of days gone by,

My mind will first revert (for memory

Would still be left) to simple kindnesses

And words of love when on my mother's knees—

The soft rebuke, that bade me not to cry,

Yet made tears fall so fast they ne'er would dry

Till kissed away, and that by slow degrees—

And later, when the spirit of the man

Grew more confiding, to those mutual looks

That led to nothing, but a heavenly thought!

And ended sweetly, just as they began,

In friendship, as we read in story books!

Love *may* be purchased; THIS can ne'er be bought.

May 22, 1888.

LADY SMITH

ON HER 100TH BIRTHDAY

I DARE not, daring much, presume to write

    On such a day mere birthday rhymes to thee !

Thou hast been chosen ! On the sheltered tree

The fruit hangs longest ; and before the Night

That must come, cometh, and the fatal blight

Reach thy ripe fruit (so mellow, yet so free

From mouldy age), accept these lines from me.

I have no claim, no vestige of a right,

To offer homage at thy peaceful shrine—

Hallowed by time, a century of worth !—

But, though unknown, I know where virtues live,

And honoured Learning makes her home divine ;

Good angels watched at thy auspicious birth—

God guard thee still, and every blessing give !

TO THE SAME

QUOTING ADDISON FROM MEMORY, IN HER 104TH YEAR

THOU wondrous Link of Time's immortal chain!
  Thou bindest Age to Age; I pray you take

The homage of a stranger: thou dost make

The roses of the Past to bloom again.

Wide-sundered founts of pleasure and of pain

Rise up for thee to form a crystal lake,

On whose strange shores Lethèan waters break,

Yet flood thy heart's warm memory in vain;

'Fountains of fire' the poet calls the Past

That memory steals to brighten present hours:

Oh! be it fire or but some silver stream,

May it be thine, dear Lady, to the last,

To illumine all around thee with its powers,

Till life ebbs slowly in an endless dream.

December 1876.

TO THE SAME

DIED IN HER 104TH YEAR

THE endless dream—the dream that has no breaking !
The dream of the Fair City's golden gates,
The white-robed throng that evermore awaits
Pure souls like thine—the dream that knows no waking
Has come at last; so slowly overtaking
Thy blessèd life, it seemed no change of states—
No cruel severance of the fabled Fates,
But a sweet passage of thine own dear making.
Borne on the wings of wisdom year by year
To brightest human points, one Heavenly Home
Was waiting for thee long—ay, long ere this.
Thou hast fulfilled thy hope, no fainting fear—
No vain regret! 'I come, dear Lord, I come,
And change earth's cares for everlasting bliss.'

February 2, 1877.

THE GOLDEN WEDDING

NOVEMBER 20, 1885

LOVE plucks a feather from the Wing of Time,
    And stays his flight to toy with centuries.
Threescore and ten! Why, half a hundred flies
In making love. The young November rime
Just whitens here and there a curl! No crime
To kiss one's wife without the subtleties
Of courtship; fifty years of married ties
Make even matrimony seem sublime!
Our Golden Wedding! Yes, the autumn sheaves
Of Golden grain are surely growing ripe,
And the rich Harvest of a well-spent life
Is ours amid the changing wintry leaves.
The chimney corner and the cheerful pipe—
Our God is good to us, dear friends and wife!

TO THE EARL OF BEACONSFIELD, K.G.

ON HIS RETURN FROM BERLIN

WHEN from the battle-field some Chief returning,

Brings back the trophies of successful war,

Though now no more to his triumphal car

Are captives chained, still hearts bereft are mourning,

And hatred and revenge are fiercely burning

In bosoms racked with sorrow : now the Star

Of Peace victorious shineth from afar,

All angry thoughts to hope and mercy turning.

No mother weeps her darling boy laid low ;

No pale-eyed maid laments her loved one slain ;

But maid and matron bless the happy day,

And weave a crown of myrtle for thy brow ;

For thou hast warred with war, turned loss to gain,

And passed in triumph from the bloodless fray.

PARIS : *July* 24, 1878.

TO THE SAME

A LOVING hand—ah! would it had been mine!—
   Has garnered, from the harvest of thy heart,
Words of true wisdom; though but meagre part
Of thy wise sayings, they are truly thine:
The thoughts are human, but a power Divine
Gives truth, and purity, and force: they start
Like natural well-springs, without visible art,
Yet art, unseen, controls; how subtly fine!
But, beyond art, the Patriot's loving soul,
Rich in the prescience of the Statesman's craft,
Baffles the braggart, and the weak defends,
Tempers wild dreams with unperceived control,
Drives falsehood forth with truth's unerring shaft,
And rich and poor in kindly union blends.

THE VOLUNTEER REVIEWS

WINDSOR AND EDINBURGH

July and August 1881

A HUNDRED thousand hearts were at thy feet,
Victoria, those two memorable days!
Thy crown, no warrior's girt with blood-stained bays,
But the fair Chaplet of Devotion, meet
To bind thy brow! while echoed every street
With arméd tramp, the city's crowded ways
Rang with the joyous war-note of thy praise;
A people's praise to thee sounds doubly sweet!
What if a kindly sun warmed Windsor's sward?
What if in Scotland fell unceasing rain?
Our Queen the storm and sunshine shared with all;
For Her, a people's love the great award,
And Her dear Country not aroused in vain,
A Volunteer Herself at duty's call.

ON DIT

THEY blame the forward glance that meets the eye

　　And does not droop the lid; they blame the maid

Whose downcast look seems modestly afraid

To own her words; no sense of chivalry

Protects from Scandal's tongue; the heart awry

Makes the vile member crookèd, or 'tis paid

To blacken innocence, and faults are laid

To this or that, unheeding the reply.

Thus strange distortions mar the fairest form,

Base motives for the noblest act are found,

Good grows to evil—in a cup of tea !—

Yet, God be praised, some stand this ribald storm

Unscathed (and on their author lies rebound),

As white-winged vessels skim a treacherous sea.

AFTER PETRARCH

AFTER PETRARCH

I

LAURA, thou fairest laurel of my crown,
  Thou leaflet ever green to my fond heart,
Not Death himself can force us twain apart,
Or daunt our spirits with his withering frown ;
If thou, pure Seraph, on bright wings hast flown
To God's own Heaven, *my* Laura still thou art,
And thou to angels canst new grace impart,
Not they to thee ; and thou art all mine own.
I follow swiftly ; but I live in thee :
And thou in me eternally shalt live.
We heed not the sharp spasm miscallèd Death,
Genius and Love make Immortality,
And thou and I to each can either give,
And blend our names in one undying wreath.

SKEFFINGTON : *February 25.*

II

WHEN I am wearied of the wavering light

Which flickers from the passions that deceive—

The lying loves—whose flames are make-believe—

I turn in peace to one serene and bright,

The fire of my own love, that through the night

Sheds its pure steadfast ray. How can I grieve,

When morn, and noon, and midnight all receive

From it a perfect radiance in my sight?

The softest breeze that plays about my brow,

Breathes its sweet fragrance from my constant love,

And the clear Heaven from it derives its blue;

'Tis some angelic Spirit whispering low

Dear words of hope that all my pains remove—

Soul of my Soul, immaculate and true!

III

IN the full summer of her beauteous prime,
  When love's rich foliage all its verdure kept,
My Laura from my circling arms was swept—
A tender blossom plucked before its time.
Was my wild love for her so great a crime,
That in the flush of life to Heaven she leapt?
Can She the eternal sleep of death have slept,
And live no more but only in my rhyme?
Why have I thus survived?   Her latest day
Had been for both the first of love renewed;
Though all unworthy, yet would I have tried
To quit all grosser attributes of clay;
And, with Her dying purity imbued,
In death for ever have been sanctified.

IN MEMORIAM

BENJAMIN DISRAELI

EARL OF BEACONSFIELD

DIED APRIL 19, 1881

I

THERE lies within the grasp of our great Foe,

One of the noblest lives that England owns—

A Man not all unused to Fortune's frowns,

Nor wasted by her smiles; whose thoughtful brow

Uniting wide extremes of high and low,

And bravely meeting all the ups and downs

Of wayward Fate—just both to Crowds and Crowns—

Grows old with grace, as only wise men grow.

Pain and disease assail him; he alone

Is unrepining; grateful for the past,

He suffers patient in that hope of Light

Which leads through darkness to the Great White Throne.

Oh, Statesmen! Patriots! he, wellnigh the last

And greatest left, desires your prayers to-night!

LONDON: *April* 16, 1881.

II

HE needs our prayers no more—no Day, no Night
Where his great soul abides.   From 'Golden Gate'
And fair 'Italian Terrace,' where but late
He walked, to Jasper Doors and Paths of Light,
And all the marvels of celestial might,
Is blessèd change for one who doubted Fate
That jars with Faith, content to work and wait
Till God shall bring His hidden things to sight.
Now we who loved him, sorrowing, bare the head,
And bend the knee before his silent grave,
And lay him down this day for evermore
To dreamless slumber in his quiet bed,
Where, after many a buffet from life's wave,
He rests at last, as on a welcome shore.

HUGHENDEN : *April* 26, 1881.

PRINCESS ALICE

ETERNAL life—God's gift—is thine to-day,
Death cowers defeated—victory is thine!
Is it not promised us, who now repine,
That the Lord God will wipe all tears away?
We part with this frail tenement of clay
And the freed spirit soars in Heaven to shine,
Elate, majestic, glorious, and Divine,
No more to wander from the perfect way.
Oh, thou pure Soul! to whom to die is gain,
Whose Earthly Crown is changed for Heavenly, send
From thy blest home, thy dwelling-place above,
Comfort to those who mourn—not all in vain
Look down once more on us who wait, and blend
Our hopes, our faith, with thy angelic love.

December 14, 1878.

TO THE SAME

IMMORTAL Love! great vanquisher of Death,
   Hast thou too yielded to his harsh demand?
Why didst thou not control the cruel hand
That decked the altar with a funeral wreath?
How could such danger lie fair flowers beneath,
And spread its desolation through the land?
What subtle poison must the Love command,
That deals destruction with its own sweet breath?
Wife, daughter, sister, mother, best in each,
Yet calmly conscious of her Princely right,
Her life to virtuous deeds was wholly given;
'Her voice yet speaketh,' and in words that teach:
A light that shineth e'en in Death's dark night,
And guides the weary wanderer to Heaven.

THE DOÑA MERCEDES DE BOURBON,

QUEEN OF SPAIN, CONSORT OF ALPHONSO XII.

MARRIED, JANUARY 23, 1878; DIED, JUNE 26, 1878; AGED 18.

ON the occasion of the marriage of King Alphonso to his young cousin, Doña Mercedes, the Author was appointed Special Ambassador at the Court of Spain. The impression made upon him, and upon those who accompanied him in his Embassy, was that the alliance was one of pure love— deep, simple, and sincere. The warm, generous disposition of the King, and the calm, serene, confiding character of his beloved bride, seemed to promise a life of domestic happiness such as Spain at all events had never witnessed in her rulers; but this was destined, as we all now know, to be cut short by the hand of Death. The incidents referred to in each sonnet actually occurred; and a letter to the Author from the King, signed 'votre affligé Alphonse,' testifies alike to the passionate depths of his love, and to the intensity of his sorrow.

I

The poor King remains leaning on her bed, and calling on her name, 'Mercedes! Mercedes mia!' To the last her eyes were turned on the King.

I have seen him twice—all he said was, 'That for him there was no consolation, but that he would do his duty.'—*Extract from a Private Letter from Madrid.*

MERCEDES MIA! turn thine eyes away,

I have no power to grant their longing prayer,

Their mute appeal is more than I can bear.

Could I but snatch thee from Death's cruel sway,

God knows how gladly I would give this day

My life for thine. For whom have I to care

When thou art gone? The darkness of despair

Clouds all my heart with terror and dismay.

Mercedes mia! I am brave once more!

My eyes will weep no more until the end,

But steadfastly, beloved, gaze in thine

Till Death arrest their sight. What! is all o'er?

Then farewell Hope! and farewell truest Friend!

Now Duty's rugged path be only mine!

II

From that window of his ancestral home, this young Monarch watched the train departing for the Escurial. Long after it had left, he continued steadily looking in the direction taken by the mortal remains of his darling bride. —*Special Correspondence of the 'Standard.'*

T HE sandy ridges of that barren plain
    (A weird wild bleakness of infinity)
Melt into space before his throbbing eye,
And his heart aches with agonising pain,
As swiftly speeds the dark funereal train,
Bearing away his Queen—too young to die—
His bride—his loyal love's idolatry—
To the Escurial's gloomy-gorgeous fane !
In the high casement of his stately home,
In tearless anguish, sits the Lord of all ;
His fixèd gaze, true as the polar star,
Points without changing to that dreary dome,
Where a thin wreath of smoke, like a grey pall,
Still guides his faithful sorrow from afar.

III

SILENCE AND TEARS

I T may be speech can ease the troubled heart,
　But there are thoughts no tongue 'can e'er express,
Thoughts drowned in tears and steeped in bitterness,
That of our inmost being form a part
Yet are unutterable.　When the strings start
And snap asunder, dumb and passionless
Fades the faint music, like a last caress,
And gone for ever is the master's art !
When the proud vessel, ere her sails be spread,
Is wrecked in port, how can I dare to say,
'Sire ! winds will grow more tranquil, and the wave
Smooth its blue back for thy Imperial tread '?
How can I choose but kneel, and humbly pray
With thee, sad Monarch, by the silent grave ?

IV

THE silent grave! Nay, leave her not among
  The marble tombs of thy ancestral dead
(Too hard a pillow for so fair a head),
But lay her tenderly where Poet's song
May consecrate thy love's undying wrong:
Where flowers and sunshine, Heaven's bright gifts, may shed
Fresh fragrance daily o'er her lonely bed,
And all her people may around her throng!
For life is but a day of work for all—
And Death is sleep—another name for rest—
Eternal rest—for Peasant or for Queen.—
So here let flowers her grace and youth recall
(Like her, short-lived, the brightest and the best),
And grief find comfort in the peaceful scene!

  July 3, 1878.

ALPHONSO XII.

Died November 25, 1885

PALE Death once more unlocks the Gloomy Gate,

    That in the dark Escurial bars the pride

And pomp of princes, and their dust doth hide

From the sweet air and light in mocking state !

Oh, cruel Death ! too soon, and yet too late,

Thou joinest once again the gentle bride

To her young lord—they now lie side by side,

Sad emblems of irrevocable Fate !

Yet are there tears for tender eyes to weep :

Tears for his country, that he loved so well,

Now left without a guide : nor tears alone ;

His watchword Duty, and the eyes, that sleep

In death, still watch.   The living then must tell

Of Duty done—not write it upon stone.

THE EARL OF IDDESLEIGH

DIED JANUARY 12, 1887

Upon sitting down to breakfast he remarked to Lord Fortescue, with
evident satisfaction, ' I shall leave no arrears.'

TRUE servant of the State, thy sudden doom—

Struck down in harness—fills the heart with grief;

Leader of men, though not perhaps the chief,

Tried both in victory and in hour of gloom,

For such as thou England has always room

And honoured welcome, resting sure belief

On deeds, not phrases, or if phrases, brief,

And words that clearly shine, not darkly loom.

Oh ! when our hour shall come, some fleeting thought

Of how thy life was spent may help us then,

Even now may help to tell, with tender tears,

Thy life of English home, greatness, unsought,

A ready sympathy for thy fellow-men,

And these brave words, ' I leave you no arrears.'

FREDERICK III. EMPEROR AND KING

JUNE 15, 1888

I

AT rest ! Thou noblest, sweetest-natured Man,
King-Emperor, Soldier, Servant of the State.

Patient in tribulation ; truly great

By God's high gift of sympathy ; in the van

Of truth and liberty, though brief the span

Of Empire given to thee ; thy tragic fate

Makes all eyes weep, for who can emulate

Thy courage stricken by so sore a ban ?

Thy gentle heart was always calm, and brave,

And cheerful in thine anguish ; but thy foe

Was still inexorable, and the Hand

That smote thee down to thy too early grave—

Alas ! in thee for evermore laid low

The truest friend of thy loved Fatherland.

II

VICTORIA ! Empress-Queen ! and widowed Wife !
    (Greater than earthly Titles is the name)
Wife worthy of thy Pure Lord—whose fame
Will·live beyond, ay, far beyond, this life !
Consort and Comforter in sorrow, rife
With untold terrors, before which grew tame
The final doom ; for, when grave words of blame
Floated in air, thy courage calmed the strife.
Loving and loved, what Greatness soothes thee now ?
No worldly honour ! but the King of Kings
Will give thee comfort ! a brief hour to wait,
To smooth the lines upon thine aching brow ;
To shelter thee beneath the Silver Wings,
And thou shalt join Him at the Golden Gate.

June 15, 1888.

* F

TO AN INFANT,

WHOSE MOTHER DIED AT ITS BIRTH

THOU guiltless-guilty, innocent-evil mite,

    With Southern hair, and Mediterranean eyes

Gazing at this cold world in sad surprise !

Hard problem thou to solve !   Can this be right,

And thy young morn be darkened with such blight

At the first dawn of life ?   Some grave surmise

Why thou shouldst suffer must perplex the wise !

No mother's arms to fold thee in the night !

Ay, babble, now, and toy with yonder flower,

Fair as thyself, and, like thy mother, born

To die in youth, and yet to leave behind

A tender seedling for some happier hour.

Thy God who sent thee here this sunny morn,

To His poor lamb will temper the harsh wind.

WORTLEY : 1882.

LADY F. C.

THINE ! all thine ! yesterday ! To-day the bride
Of Death !—The king who dominates our life—
Seizes our unweaned babes, and tears the wife
From the new-wedded arms, where love and pride
Seemed strong enough his menace to deride,
But yet were powerless in the fatal strife.
Earth teems with sorrow; every day is rife
With such grim terror as the Erl-king's ride.
Yes, she has left you—passionless—unstrung—
Like the mute viol—all your music fled—
But not for long; we follow on the track
That Poets through all time have sadly sung—
The track of starlit paths—of happy dead,
And mourn her here, but may not wish her back.

October 2, 1881.

F 2

ADMIRAL ROUS

DIED JUNE 19, 1877, AGED 82

And though men be so strong that they come to fourscore years, yet is
their strength then but labour and sorrow.

L ABOUR and sorrow! Nay, at fourscore years
    No sorrow bowed his venerable head,
No labour daunted or discomfited;
His heart was young, his spirit knew no fears.
The sorrow now is ours, and ours the tears
By eyes unused to weep—now freely shed.
The merry hours, the happy days are fled,
Yet each some fond undying memory bears.
And fourscore years of faithful duty done,
Of high-souled honour, and of friendship, set
On rock foundations, are not vainly spent;
These train a generation scarce begun,
And teach a moral none should e'er forget—
'To live uprightly is to die content.'

GEORGE WHYTE-MELVILLE

KILLED HUNTING, DEC. 5, 1878

THE engineer by his own petard slain,

    The eagle pierced by shaft from his own wing,

Are plaintive fancies, such as poets sing,

And touch the heart but coldly, through the brain.

But thou, dear George, in thine own sport thus ta'en

In all the prime of manhood, and the swing

Of gallant gallop struck stone-dead—the thing

Appals, and petrifies the mind with pain.

Bright, brave, and tender, Poesy's pet child,

Romance and History's lore alike were thine;

Thy wit ne'er wounded, yet the contest won,

For at thy jest the gravest dullard smiled—

Last scion of an ancient Scottish line,

Whose 'old folks' live to mourn their only Son.

December 6, 1878.

CHISLEHURST

DEAD! my one Boy—my only one; and Dead.
      Sirs, do not mock me—say it is not so.
He was the hope of France—nay, let me go,
I am his mother; life cannot be fled
From those young eyes, and that belovèd head
That should have worn a Crown: a Crown of woe
Truly I wear for him—though fallen so low,
An Empress still, dethroned and banishèd.
I crave your pardon: now I cannot weep,
Henceforth I weep for ever; gone! all gone!
Throne, Husband, Child, all snatched away from me;
A childless widow prays you, Sirs, to keep
Some kind thoughts for her. She is all alone,
Her heart is broken by much misery.

June 22, 1882

LORD LYTTON

THE feebleness that drags the soul to earth,
    And clogs the brain, and clips the soaring wings,
Palsies the tongue that charms, the voice that sings,
Is man's sad heritage—emblem of his birth.
There is to some a power Divine, whose worth
Is strength in weakness—whose enchantment brings
A life beyond the clay—far nobler things
Than rest or unrest, melancholy or mirth.
These were thy gifts—excelling in them all.
The young grew wise beneath thy wizard touch,
The old bloomed young again; Death lost his sway,
For Genius mocks his ineffective thrall!
All praise be thine—and yet not overmuch—
Thy fame—the dawning of an endless day.

ARCHIBALD CAMPBELL TAIT

ARCHBISHOP

THE chalice of thy holy life is dry!
    Already sounds the Angel's welcome voice
That bids thee hasten home: 'Rejoice, rejoice!
The saints rejoice whenever good men die!'
Oh Servant of the Lord! thy fearless eye
Now weeps no more! such death had been thy choice—
No cruel pang to shake the equipoise
Of thy true-balanced mind in agony!
Thy thoughts, perchance, turned to the heathery haunts
Of childhood, whence thy simple Bible-lore,
That raised thee to the highest throne of Priest.
Then, smiling (for no dying terror daunts
Such hearts), he passed to loved ones gone before,
Who waited for him; Greatest, and yet Least!

Advent Sunday, 1882.

R. F. B.,

LIEUT.-COL. GRENADIER GUARDS

DIED OF HIS WOUND RECEIVED AT TEL-EL-KEBIR, OCT. 23, 1882

TO fall full-front to foe—a soldier's death—
    For this our pride may glisten through our tears ;
But to lie wounded, racked with hopes and fears,
And slowly feel the sword wear out the sheath :
In life's rich prime to yield the joyous breath
That fanned his flame so brightly ; with such years
Of Hope (foul flatterer, he now appears)
To twine fresh foliage in thy Victor's Wreath ;—
Ay ! this is cruel—and thus hast thou died !
Alas ! how near the Glory and the Grave,
The shout of triumph and the tombstone phrase,
Cypress and Laurel ever side by side,
Prayer-hallowed tears, yet all in vain to save,
And what thou ne'er canst hear—thy Country's praise !

October 29, 1882.

74

LORD RAVENSWORTH

DIED 1878

THOU greatly gifted! yet not well content
    To idly rest on Nature's gifts alone,
But resolute for victory, as one
Who learns the art of fence, on war intent,
Thy sword is chosen without stain or dent
From learning's armoury, and its blade has shone
In peaceful strife; thy deeds of fame are done
In classic joust and poet's tournament.
How gladly would I carry helm and spear,
A willing Squire to such a valiant Knight,
And couch a lance in this most glorious fray,
Where all who fight, each one to each, grow dear!
They welcome truth and beauty as the light
Of triumph—pure as Heaven's eternal day.

September 6, 1874.

MRS. E. BARRETT BROWNING

STRONG-HEARTED lover of the sore-oppressed!
  Thou sleepest now by Arno's wayward stream;
And in that sleep perchance thy life's fond dream
Of comfort for the suffering haunts thy rest;
Still wouldst thou grasp lone children to thy breast,
Still wouldst thou make earth's blessings richly teem
For those who want, nor judge things as they seem,
Nor choose the path of riches, for the best.
Through a sad life of duty nobly done
Rose the rich music of thy Poet-voice
For struggling childhood. Sleep serenely now,
The fight is o'er! the victory is won!
Through pain and tears, the saddest hearts rejoice
To weave the eternal laurel for thy brow!

TO ROBERT BROWNING

WEIRD thinker-out of thoughts beyond the ken
　　Of common mortals, rugged though sublime ;
Probing the inmost depths of farthest time,
Audacious—wielding thy inscrutable pen
Like flashing falchion, dazzling thoughtless men
By thy thoughts' force, compressed in strange-wrought
　　rhyme.
Few feet can follow where thou lov'st to climb,
To eagle's eyrie or to lion's den !
Oh ! Master (not unaided in thy song
By her who sleepeth now near Arno's wave,
Worthy to help thee, or with thee to write),
Deign to instruct us weaker ones, who long
To rest their wavering thoughts—not wholly brave—
Where through the obscure there shines more perfect light !

BYRON

A MIND diseased? Nay, rather, out of tune,
Like some fine instrument in cruel hands;
A little tenderness the tone commands,
And a rough touch (like wintry winds in June)
Checks the true note, and turns the music soon
To discord: so he wandered through strange lands
And 'all his sweet bells jangled,' and he stands
An outcast, tainted i' th' full o' th' moon!
Oh that such madness were more common! none
To make it or to mar it—genius, such
As his, driven to revolt by meaner soul,
That knew not what it meddled with! Ne'er shone
The sun on nobler heart; but, overmuch
His spirit vexed, lost hope and self-control.

ABDUL-AZIZ

WHAT Oriental Despot now can claim
    Ancestral privilege of ruling ill?
What Western Monarch throned on people's will
Can boast his kingdom safe, with evil name?
None! They must rest their lives on noble fame
And honest deeds, lights set upon a hill,
That all may see a prudent ruler's skill;
Clear eyes averted from all deed of shame,
And hearts that win love—monarchs are but men.
Thus may they nobly keep their high estate,
Nor hear the grovelling sycophants deride!
Thrones totter to their base and fall—what then?
A nation's curses and a nation's hate,
Flight—the assassin's knife, or suicide!

TYROLEAN SONNETS

AND OTHER SONNETS OF TRAVEL

TYROLEAN SONNETS

I

THERE is a noble beauty in this land,
     Where Nature revels in contrasting grace,
For smile and frown change quickly on her face,
And tender touches soften the rough hand.
Gaunt precipice and rock, sublimely grand,
Melt into valley; and the tinkling trace
Of bell-clad herds enlivens many a space
That spreads a carpet where grim mountains stand.
The plains are faint with cyclamen and thyme,
The gloomy pines their pungent odours lend,
The gentian robs the heaven of half its blue,
Light harebells—tuneful as the poet's rhyme—
Nod in the breeze, and alpine roses blend,
    Pink as the morn, to make one perfect hue.

II

HIGH o'er the crag the poisèd eagle flics,
    And croaking ravens to each other call:
Bloodscenters both, they see the chamois fall,
And taste the banquet ere the victim dies.
They heed not the big tear that dews his eyes,
Ere filmed by death—the hunter's fatal ball
More kind than they—revolting festival!
Yet Nature to her children simply cries.
The bullfinch, mid the fir-tree's scented cones,
Whistles his happy song; the cautious hind,
Half hid among the heather, sniffs the air,
Tainted by man, and hides her little ones
In mossy dell, protected by the wind
That warns them of the foe who nears her lair.

October 2, 1887.

III

THE WATERFALL OF GASTEIN BY MOONLIGHT

THE shimmer of the Moon has lit the Vale
    And tipt the fir-tops with a silvery light,
Herself invisible; the Landscape, bright
With hidden ray, is wonderfully pale!
A spell seems cast around; some Ghostly tale
Of spectral glamour, or weird second-sight,
Would well assist this Tyrolean night
To make strong hearts beat fast, and weak ones quail.
The radiance deepens as the Planet springs
Above the mountain, and the streams, aglow
With her sweet kisses, woo the Waterfall,
Which, for one kiss, ten thousand backward flings—
A prodigal of love—and mystic echoes throw
A deep resounding music over all.

GASTEIN : *September* 3, 1887.

IV

ON THE RAILWAY BETWEEN ZÜRICH AND INNSBRUCK

WHAT prescient mind devised these gradients? laid
      These daring curves, that tempt the unwary shock?
And through these gates of immemorial rock
Carved iron roads, and pleasant pathways made?
Not soft Romance nor Conquest; but sleek Trade—
That the fine words of Poesy loves to mock,
And on bright Fancy turns prosaic lock—
Triumphed o'er Nature with her own dear aid!
For day by day, unconsciously, there came
All beauty, grace of form, and dignity,
Peak above Peak snowclad, or tender green
Peeping through some sweet Vale without a name,
Forest on Forest rising to the Sky,
And Rivulets rushing through the unrivalled scene.

August 28, 1887.

V

THE PRIEST AT GASTEIN

IF pleasure were the aim and end of all,
    And Life, so called, to be the final bound
Of my existence; then this thrilling sound—
Tumultuous music of the waterfall
At play for ever with the rocks—might call
My days to poesy, and this spangled ground,
Where Nature's fairest offerings abound,
Might be my couch, and they at last my Pall.
But the proud prodigal Earth is not my home,
Nor the dark Forest my abiding place:
These passing blooms but captivate the eye.
The closer sanctuary needs me, and I come
To guide a wayward and rebellious race
To Him who bore His Cross to Calvary.

VI

THE HAYMAKERS

A NARROW cliff, above a narrower stream,
    Spanned by a single arch, led gently down
By paths, that children, wandering from the Town
In search of berries for the rich man's cream,
Had partly worn, to where a sunny gleam
Lit up the Fir-tree's unrelenting frown,
And a broad meadow all alive with brown
Quaint figures shone out—sudden as a gleam.
No carpet ever owned the varied hues
That lavish Nature here profusely spread,
And dancing sunbeams made the tints more gay ;
Pink cyclamen and tender gentian blues
Clustered 'mid feathery grasses 'neath the tread
Of these brown Peasants busy with their Hay !

HOMBURG

I KNOW a nook beneath a sheltered hill,
  Sheltered from summer's glare or winter's wind,
Whence the far-seeing eye may hardly find
A boundary, its feeble span to fill,
So vast the billowy plain, which spreads, until
The purple hills, forming their ranks behind,
Squadron on squadron, daunt the gazer's mind
With their recurrent shapes, so grand and still,
So distant yet so visible.   Could they
Descend in serried order, each 'gainst each,
And multiply by millions, the dread blast
Of the Archangel's trump might guide the fray
And stir such hosts to scale the deadly breach:
But while I gazed, the wondrous Vision passed!

August 7, 1877.

MONT BLANC

ONCE more, great Teacher, at thy feet I rest,
    Once more I gaze upon thy storm-clad brow,
Now lustrous in fresh covering of snow,
That like a mane floats from thy thunderous crest.
As from some hoary sage, whose wisdom best
Springs from green heart, thy lessons also flow
From bosom where green things eternal grow,
And head whose whiteness Heaven itself hath prest.
Thirty long years have fled since first I came
To worship thee, a lad whose fondest hopes
Have come and gone in undeserved success;
Still lingers faintly the perfervid flame
Of youth—renewed while loitering on thy slopes,
Sublimest shrine of Nature's holiness!

CHAMOUNIX: *August* 28, 1876.

LAUTERBRUNNEN

OH GOD! Thy gracious works are manifest
    In Desert and in City; Plain and Hill
Alike declare Thy omnipresent skill;
Yet here, if anywhere, they seem the best;
These giant mountains, at their base, caressed
By tender turf and gently rippling rill;
The rose-hued snow, sunlit, or at Thy will
Storm-blackened, veiling their untrodden crest;
The feathery pines that point to Thee, the spray
That kisses the gaunt rock from yonder fall,
The resonant bells attuned by browsing kine,
The fair-haired children by the grassy way,
The sturdy mountaineer's re-echoing call—
Thou seest all are good, and all are Thine!

August 22, 1876.

DAYBREAK IN PARIS

THE rosy gleam of newly kindled day
    Just tips yon gilded Dome, as Paris wakes,
Before the lingering stars depart, or breaks
The full-orbed morning, *débonnaire* and gay :
The country wains, with loads of fragrant hay,
Creep slowly in, and Norman ' Surefoot' makes
His bell-clad head-gear jingle, as he takes
A sly bite, half in earnest, half in play.
Thus, while late sleepers dream, the busy toil
To feed the idle—and the blue-smocked clown
Is happier far than they who glove their hands.
His sweet-breathed hay to him is better spoil
Than ill-got gold, his team worth all the town,
And his fair France the bravest of all lands.

PARIS : *July* 28, 1878.

A STORM AT SEA

G REAT clouds, like war-ships, speed athwart the sky;

    On the white drift a close-reefed mainsail, gleams;

The savage blast through the taut cordage screams,

Or fitful moans with melancholy cry;

Around, the raging waters foaming lie

In frenzied wrath, and not a sun-ray beams.

The mother, in her broken slumber, dreams

Of her dear sailor, shuddering lest he die!

Ocean runs riot! and the bruisèd waves

Are blue and green with overmastering blows;

The tangled weeds, disturbed, torn from their bed

A hundred fathoms down 'mid sailors' graves,

Toss here and there, as light as fresh-fall'n snows,

And dismal caves disgorge their prisoned dead.

INSIDE PARIS

THEY banquet on dead bodies, like the ghouls,

    Who, tasting blood, grow dainty, and refuse

More wholesome diet: could these maniacs choose

Once more, their choice would be the same; mad fools

Who manacle fair Freedom; wretched tools,

Mixed up with felons, scum of men, who use

The plots of hell, and wrong with right confuse,

To push their lawful rulers from their stools:

These are the cowards who refuse to fight

A foreign foe, and soil the sacred name .

Of Country with her children's gore, who burn

The proudest trophies of imperial might;

Who marshal harlots in the ranks of fame,

And honest men's undying hatred earn.

October 24, 1878.

LILLESHALL ABBEY

THE old walls echo with their careless mirth;
  The clustering ivy forms fantastic frame
Of mingled root and branch round carven name
And porch indented at its Norman birth.
The Abbot, more for rank renowned than worth,
Sleeps calmly through the centuries, his fame
Akin to modern reputations. Praise and blame
Alike return to whence they came—the earth.
Unmindful of such thoughts, three children fair,
Hand clasped in hand, run laughing through the aisle,
Nor reck the Abbot's fate, though surely theirs;
The fourth, a twelvemonth old to-day, crows in the air
Responsive welcome to her mother's smile—
Of time and destiny unconscious Heirs.

August 5, 1886.

BURGHLEY HOUSE

WHERE great Eliza's ghost austerely stalks,
    I dwell: a sojourner in Burghley Park;
And, even as strangers more acutely mark
The shifting of Life's scenes than he who walks
Serenely day by day, and careless talks
Of this or that plain thing, so with the Lark
Uprising at the Dawn, and to the Dark
Observing, nought my clear perception balks.
Then first, oh, Virgin Queen, I make to thee
Profound obeisance; then to Thee whose nod
Spake volumes, and whose simple word gave law;
And then to those who hold their memory
In reverence, grateful to the Gracious God
Who kept them their good name without a flaw.

July 17, 1882.

CALVARY

AND OTHER SONNETS OF MEDITATION

CALVARY

THE mocking gibe! the cruel taunt! if heard,
    Unanswered by the lips now sealed in death;
The last sigh breathed in love; the parting breath
A prayer for pardon for that bitter word.
'He savèd others!' as the parent bird
Gives her own life to save the young beneath
Her loving wing; He died—the immortal wreath
For others wreathed—by suffering undeterred.
'Himself He cannot save!' Omnipotent,
He would not use this power—the angel's sword—
That could have saved the Saviour, at the cost
Of man's redemption, and His mission spent
In vain! Thou Son of Man! Divinest Lord!
What had we sinners been—Thou saved, we lost?

H

'ORA E SEMPRE!'

'ORA E SEMPRE!' when the morn of life
  Bursts from rose-tinted clouds in eastern skies,
And all the promise of their radiant dyes
With hope, and mirth, and revelry is rife.
'Ora e sempre!' when our manhood's strife
Wrestles within, and sterner duty tries
The heart's wild passion, with grey pitiless eyes
And cuts it from us with relentless knife.
'Ora e sempre!' every moment shows
The need for action or for earnest will,
For patient suffering or for sympathy
That, scorning self, with generous impulse glows;
And when our Sun sets, calm, and cold, and still,
'Ora e sempre' in Eternity!

THE KNIGHTHOOD OF THE CROSS

THERE is a Knightly Order, nobler far
　　Than all the ranks of Chivalry can claim—
An order founded not on earthly fame,
Not decked with jewelled blazon or with star,
Not graced by trophies or triumphal car—
It is the Cross of Christ, whose lowly name
Puts pride to blush and vanity to shame—
The Prince of Peace who only wars with war.
Love is the sweet esquire of Christ's true knight,
And Death 'Grand Master,' whose austere embrace
Chills the warm heart and checks the joyous breath
But for a moment—then the Neophyte,
Inspired and glorious, gives, with radiant face,
The kiss of Life—the Accolade of Death!

Christmas Day, 1878.

GOETHE'S PRAYER

'MORE Light, more Light,' the Poet's plaintive prayer
  Ere his eyes close for ever in Death's night!
The fainting supplication for ' more Light,'
No common struggle for a purer air,
But temporal and eternal joining there!
He prays for rescue from the awful night
Of Doubt, that daunts the soul, and blinds the sight,
And makes all dark, that should be bright and fair.
'More Light, more Light,' in life to Thee we pray,
Great God! Wise Man, to Thee! (Creator Thou,
Created in His image thou), this cry
Of dying Goethe; in our earthly day,
The light of knowledge—truth with open brow—
And God's own Light to guide us when we die.

NOT HERE

LAST week I saw the lilac's budding leaf ;
This week I see the lilac's buds all strewn,
The leaflets scattered, and the bloom o'erthrown
By sudden icy blasts as chill as grief.
Such promise marred, like faith by unbelief,
Such hope destroyed without a warning word,
Like the flushed revellers by the impending sword,
Where may we turn in anguish for relief?
Not Here ; for east winds freeze the heart—not Here !
But where eternal summers blossom—there
Where God's unchanging seasons bring sure fruit,
In the pure climes of Heaven, Blessèd Sphere,
Where radiant suns are present everywhere,
And Heavenly Hands protect the tender shoot.

TRUE REST

WHAT do men long for, strive for, live for most?
The purple mantle of ambitious dreams?
The lying gold that clouds the fairest streams?
The sacred fervour that adores the Host?
In all pure nature's simple love is lost,
And truth is farthest when it nearest seems.
Oh, Earth! thy bosom with corruption teems,
And war meets war, and none e'er counts the cost.
Great Heaven, how just are Thy decrees to all!
How seeming hard to some! For faith I pray,
For truth and for content; then death is blest;
Then virtue, silver-crowned, spreads out our pall,
And all our life is patent as the day,
And after labour comes Seraphic Rest.

HEAVENLY HARVEST-HOME

THERE is no constancy in things below,
  There must be constancy in things above—
Above, below, our prize is ever Love;
From Heavenly plants divinest blossoms blow.
If earthly love melts like the spring-tide snow,
Pure while it lasts, it still is Treasure-trove,
Which the glad finder scarce knows how to prove,
Till time cuts short the branches ere they grow.
But time o'er Heavenly love has no control;
And after Time has reaped, God's gleaner comes,
And, loving all, garners each downcast ear.
From the torn stalk, divides the longing soul,
And gathers it to those glad Harvest-homes
Where hearts are purified, and eyes see clear.

1860.

LIGHT

IF in the darkness of to-morrow's day,

    And in the dim obscure that veils the hours,

I own the presence of those shadowy powers

That sport with reason, and with judgment play;

I feel it less when some warm sunny ray

Dispels the menace of disheartening showers;

But when thick mist or angry storm-fiend lowers,

My spirits in bleak regions lonely stray.

Then grant me beams, kind Heaven, from above,

To glad a heart that ever seeks the Light;

Disperse the clouds that gather round the mind;

Let Sunshine bring his comrades, Peace and Love,

And daunt the sable messengers of Night:

In Light I see, in Darkness grow stone-blind!

1861.

WORDS OF COMFORT AT CHRISTMAS

RED ROWAN, like the Robin's breast aglow,
　　And scarlet-berried Holly all aflame,
And wax-white Mistletoe, whose childhood came
And grew in alien branches—tipped with snow
As light as swans-down that a breath might blow :—
These—ten small fingers (deftly trained to tame
The stubborn shoots) twined with The Holy Name,
And words of comfort sorrowing sufferers know :—
'Come unto Me,' for this is Christmas Tide,
'All ye who labour and are laden, come,'
This is Christ's birthday !—He, the Christ, who died
To bid us welcome to His Heavenly Home !
Oh ! words to mourning hearts for ever blest,
'Come unto Me, and I will give you rest !'

October 12, 1884.

THY PLACE IS KEPT FOR THEE

THY place is kept for thee.   What though the scorn
  Of cruel men may give thy heart some pain?
Thy loss in that is no loss—rather gain—
And leads through night to an eternal morn.
Deep in thy bleeding bosom is the thorn,
And thoughts unspeakable may rack thy brain;
But still thy place is kept, and once again
Thou shalt be pure, as thou wert purely born.
Thy place is kept for thee, if only thou
Wilt seek it sorrowing, barefoot, and in tears,
The Crown of penance on thy forehead; then
Thou wilt discover that thy wounded brow
A sweeter solace for its anguish bears,
And God will keep thy place, in spite of men.

APRIL 30, 1881

SMILE on us, ancient Abbey, grim and grey,
    The gentle smile of all-forgiving age!
Write one more story on your time-worn page;
Blow, sweet south wind, upon this happy day,
Break into leaf, 'ye darling buds of May!'
Love reigns supreme—a service without wage,
Where all are willing, Senator and Sage
Bend to the flowery yoke, and own his sway:
Ring out, old bells, and welcome this dear pair,
Who join their hands this day in life-long troth;
God's blessing rest upon their faithful love!
Fulfil their joyous dreams, make their life fair,
Smooth its rough places tenderly for both,
And, parted here, renew their bliss above!

PATHETIC HUMOUR

THERE is no limit fixed by God or man
      Between our laughter and our tears: the touch
Of nature, tinged with pathos overmuch,
Fills the soft heart and ready eyes that scan,
With unresisting glance, the subtle plan
That melts or moves to laughter.   There be such
Whose truth, half-halting, borrows Fiction's crutch
The chasm of our credulity to span!
But when enlisted in the ranks of right,
Of want relieved, and suffering and wrong
Made good by noble deeds and thoughts and words,
Our simple hearts o'erflow, the pulse of might
Beats stronger, and sometimes to these belong
Great gifts of Humour sharper than all swords.

DEAD

I KNOW not what I write, the pen must frame
  The words that rush in heart-leaps from my soul;
No rhythmic cadence in well-ordered roll,
But passionate thoughts that have nor place nor name;
These are not lines aglow for future fame,
Rounded to please, smooth-smirking and heart-whole,
But wild with sorrow that defies control,
And anguish time can neither heal nor tame:
We were one age, one hope, one life, one dream,
She fair as Dawn's first rose-beam on the snow;
We parted—but to meet at break of day;
For her the day ne'er broke, the eternal stream
Bore her sweet soul on its resistless flow,
And left me on the brink in dumb dismay.

November 13, 1878.

DROWNED

CAN danger lurk beneath that placid wave,
  Where the great lazy water-lilies float
In safe and careless beauty? where the throat
Of warbling sedge-bird from his reedy cave
Swells with a joyous song—where still streams lave
The grassy banks? Can these such ills denote,
Or presage peril to the little boat?
Can lilied crystal be a maiden's grave?
Alas! we know not what may be the fate
Of hapless hundreds,[1] or the doom of one!
Our tears alone are left us, and we shed
Tears from a fount that never dries; too late,
Yet all too soon—our children come—are gone—
And we are left to mourn the darlings dead.

September 1878.

[1] On this day occurred the disaster to the *Princess Alice* steamer in the Thames.

FORGET-ME-NOT

'HAST thou no loving message from thy tomb,
    Dear Father? Sleepest thou in mute decay,
Silently waiting for that awful day
When the great Judge of all shall speak our doom?
Is there no light with thee? doth cheerless gloom
Compass thee ever? If thou canst, oh! say
Thou restest peacefully, though far away
From this fair earth—its sunlight and its bloom.'
I yearned to hear some voice; but none replied
Save the rich note of the new-wedded thrush,
Who carolled over-joyous with his lot;
When, as I gazed on the dear grave, I spied
A little blue flower softly whispering, 'Hush!
My name is thy reply—*Forget-me-not!*'

May 1878.

SYMPATHY IN FRIENDSHIP

THE tone of a soft voice—a tender smile
    That in our happy moments bears its part—
The inexplicable yearning of the heart
For some dear face, a stranger to all guile,
A face wrath ne'er can cloud, guilt ne'er defile,
Nor sorrow darken, save for others' smart!
Such faces their own purity impart,
And teach true sympathy; the cunning wile,
That makes pretence of feeling for the pain
And grief of others, like a mirror gleams,
Whose light reflects each dull contiguous face.
Thus friendship in true sympathy grows plain,
And sympathy in friendship fondly beams:
False friends, false sympathy, make one disgrace.

THE GATES OF DEATH

WE enter Life but through the gates of Death,
Those dismal portals cinctured by a moat—
A flood of human tears; vile passions gloat
And glare on us like gurgoyles, with rank breath,
And eyes aflame, around, above, beneath.
But God's good angel guides our little boat,
That safely homewards seems unsteered to float,
With sword of fire uplift, full-drawn from sheath.
Safe, safe at last, from doubt, from storm, from strife,
Moored in the depths of Christ's unfathomed grace
With spirits of the just, with dear ones lost
And found again; this strange ineffable life
Is Life Eternal! Death has here no place,
And they are welcomed best who suffered most.

Christmas Day, 1878.

MIDDLE AGE

THY glory is the glory of the sun,
  Whose chastened beauty in the twilight glows,
And tenderer yet, and yet more tender, grows,
As nearer to the goal his course is run—
The farewell Glory of a day nigh done—
Then all the peaks assume a tint of rose,
And the grey rocks a ruddy light disclose,
The blush of Even at her victory won.
How calm, how peaceful, such a moment's rest!
Not wooing love with passionate desire,
But placid—perfect in mature repose.—
Such, Lady, are thy charms, by all confest:
Past the meridian glare, the summer fire,
Yet, oh, how far from winter's dreary snows!

September 6, 1874.

OLD AGE

THERE is a beauty Youth can never know,
  With all the lusty radiance of his prime,
A beauty the sole heritage of time,
That gilds the fabric with a sunset glow,
And glorifies the work it soon lays low!
There is a charm in Age, wellnigh sublime,
That lends new lustre to the poet's rhyme,
As mountain-peaks are grander crowned with snow.
How gay the laugh of Youth! but oh! how brave
The stately weakness of a reverend Age!
Be ours the task to solace and to cheer,
To fondly guide its footsteps to the grave,
To print a blessing on the final page,
And cherish memories for ever dear!

THE TRIUMPHS OF LITERATURE

'TIS the last straw that breaks the camel's back,'
    I've read I know not where, nor care to ask—
So, trembling lest thy strength it overtask,
I lay this little straw upon thy Pack
Laden with priceless gems through the long track
Of centuries, since Learning tore the mask
From Vice and Ignorance. Be it mine to bask
One moment in thy Light—all else how black!
No people claim thy triumphs as their own—
Italia, Greece, the swarthy Orient, all
Are but thy slaves to-day, or yesterday.
Thou laugh'st at Time; all Languages have grown
From thee; thine Eden's grace and Eden's fall,
All rose from thee, and cannot pass away.

1882.

LIFE AND DEATH

HOW can I purify my soul from dross
    That poisons hearts with its impure alloy?
How gain eternal, craving passing, joy?
How sue for heavenly, dreading earthly, loss?
Rough winds and rougher seas may wildly toss
My little bark, that like a painted toy
Rides the dark waters, when such storms annoy;
But Death must surely some day 'swim the foss.'
Ah, then, how vain are all Life's troublous dreams!
How poor our struggle, and how mean our strife!
How bleak the past! the present, ah! how dread,
When Death's bright sunset like a glory gleams,
And for this fleeting we gain endless Life!
Oh! who could choose to be for ever dead?

ALONE

I SAW the sun obscured, the lightning dart
　　Its forkèd tongue from out a sable cloud;
The big drops fell, the thunder boomed aloud,
And the dread sounds found echo in my heart.
My heart, that, like the sun, had found rich part
In the full glow of summer, here was cowed
By the dark noisome shadow of the crowd
That thronged my loved one, like a thing i' the mart.
The thunder ceased to roar—the crowd passed by,
The lightning faintly faded in the west,
The rain dried up its tears, as quickly gone
As shed; the sun once more shone lustily—
My heart leapt out to her whom I loved best,
But ah! in vain, for I was left Alone.

THE DISCONTENTED

THERE are, who in this changing life revile
　　The day-by-day occurrences they meet—
Turn sweet to bitter, ay, make bitter sweet,
Rather than be content and wear a smile.
To these no fair occasions offer; for unfair
All circumstance appears: the sun shines wrong,
The rain is foolish, time itself too long,
The air inclement—victims everywhere!
Oh! could they see, as I have seen, the poor,
Racked by real anguish, worn by want and pain,
Contented bend, and humbly kiss the rod,
Perchance they too might seek the cottage door
And learn a lesson to their endless gain—
And for His constant mercies thank their God.

ABANDONED

MINSTREL of minstrelsy too false for me;
Coiner of coinage never more to pass;
Singer of songs, whose voice is sounding brass;
Heedless no more, I heed—but heed not thee.
Framer of frames where portraits ought to be;
Schemer of schemes all brittle as a glass;
Swearer of oaths too well believed, alas!
Slavish no more, I slave—but not for thee.
Liars like thee at last must lie in vain,
Dreamers like me must cease to dream at last.
Too credulous, I doubt, and doubt for ever;
And the vile anguish of my endless pain
Remembered always, though the shock be past,
Perforce from me all faith, all love, must sever.

LOVE IN AGE

THE boon of Age, when Love has taken flight,
    And left us a stray feather from his wing
To play with, is a tender heart, to bring
The memory of the truant to our sight!
Not what we are, but what perchance we might,
With some kind help, be ; a convenient thing
That serves to play with, yet the bitter sting
Of grey-haired failure never brought to light!
Ah, me ! the rosy lips of careless youth
That vanquished, ignorant of the art of war,
The words that were a library—the sighs
That seemed a malady—and all in truth—
And now, the careful handshake from afar,
And subtle glances that are mostly lies!

WOMAN'S FATE

AND has it come to this? the suppliant rules,
And all his vows are scattered on the wind;
He knows his power, and once so cruel-kind,
Girds at me now as taught in meaner schools,
And with contempt scarce veiled calls women fools,
And cries, 'Not I, 'twas thou—so loving-blind,
How couldst *thou* guess the workings of my mind?'
They cut their hands who play with keen-edged tools:
Just Heaven! can trifling with a woman's heart
Bring down no judgment on the trifler? Say,
When he implored, knelt, pleaded, promised all,
Was I to blame who trusted him with part,
Though 'twere the greater part? Must such as they
Stand scathless, and the true ones only fall?

PAST AND PRESENT

THE time is past! What time? The time for good?

    Nay, that can ne'er be past; the stream flows on;

The silver dimples of the wave are gone;

But other waves succeed in endless flood.

The time is come! What time? Here's ample food

For meditation: neither time alone,

The Past or Present, ever can atone

For future wrong, or heal a sickly mood.

The time will come—ay, time will come indeed—

And for that time the bravest must prepare—

When black Past, blacker—bright, still brighter seems;

Ah, then, how keenly search we for some deed,

To ease our dying souls of load of care,

And gild our Present with its golden beams!

    1860.

DISAPPOINTMENT

THROUGH the long vigil of a sleepless night
    To watch and listen for the chime of morn,
To mark the splendour of the day new-born,
When all the Orient flushes into light;
To cry 'half-won,' and, radiant with delight,
To laugh the heart's forebodings all to scorn—
To fling aside the rose, and plant the thorn,
Unconsciously, in confidence of might:
Then, lo! grey mist obscures the glowing sun,
The hand, unnerved, lets fall the staff it grasped,
The exultant voice sounds hoarse, and choked, and low,
And Triumph fails before her course be run;
And Victory, ere the precious prize be clasped,
In Disappointment veils her downcast brow.

1856.

OLD PRINTS

IN A PORTFOLIO

THEY lie within this purgatorial book,

In patient waiting for the Day of Doom,

As lost, as labour of the Tyrian loom,

This courtly smile, or that imperious look !

Here simpers Phyllis with a flowery crook,

And there frowns one who sought the cannon's boom,

And courted peril, as a mistress, whom

He madly worshipped, and by yonder brook

A loving pair stand gazing into space—

They whisper fondly of their future home,

Though dead a hundred years !   A cruel fate

Is theirs indeed, each packed within this case—

Unhappy prisoners in a dusty tome

That closes o'er them like the Inferno's Gate !

SUDDEN ANGER

HOW often have I seen a cloudless sky
  In the full noontide of supreme repose,
When the far distant hills were flushed with rose
And nature slept in drowsy lethargy,
In a moment darken, while an ominous cry
Of rising wind, with strange parturient throes,
Rings through the foliage; and with angry blows
A sudden tempest tosses all awry.
So, o'er the trusting heart's delusive calm,
When all seems peaceful, prosperous, and fair,
Have I seen sudden storms, like whirlwinds, driven:
No certain peace, no penitential psalm,
To smooth the passionate pilgrim's path of care:
Only one hope—one prayer—to be forgiven.

May 5, 1885.

DEAD LOVE

IN the hot South a little fleecy cloud
In summer sky unfelt a tempest makes :
So in a sunny life some Demon takes
Fierce hold, and shattered Love lies in her shroud ;
Love, in Death's arms, faint, pitiful, and cowed.

Ah ! cruel sight ! my sick heart well-nigh breaks ;
The trustful smile her pallid lip forsakes ;
Her robe is torn, her beauty disallowed.

Is there no Philtre that can bid her live?
No unguent that can heal her present pain?
No charm to fan once more her fragrant breath ?

Ask if the winds and waves their foes forgive.
They may—but I can never love again
And leave my lost love in the arms of Death.

THE EVENING OF LIFE

HOW do we measure life ? how shape our ends
  To judge the flight of time, and our decay,
The rapid passage of our little day ?
By growth of children, and by death of friends,
Pushed from our places, as the first extends,
We smile to see our offspring at their play,
And willingly for those we love, make way,
Trusting their lives, for ours, may make amends !
But for the tell-tale sorrows that surround
The agèd ! nay, the middle-aged—who see
Still younger friends cut down, as leaves are shed
In some spring gale and cumber the damp ground—
There are no words of comfort; if there be,
Go seek them in the Service for the Dead.

April 29, 1887.

1884

IN EXTREMIS

A FEW more moments and the fateful hour
    That ends his feeble sway must come: so near!
The bells are tolling, and I seem to hear
The stroke of Doom that terminates his power,
And gives another the transcendent dower
Of world-wide empire over Love and Fear—
Love that rules all but time, and dries the tear
He often makes to flow—a passing shower!—
With palpitating pinion, lighting down
From Seraph-region, stands the wistful Heir
Of all things earthly.   Be with him to-night,
Oh God of mercy !   Black as it be grown,
Turn the past white, make smooth the brow of care,
And guide Thy children for this year aright.

December 31, 1884, 12 P.M.

CONSCIENCE

HIDE thee within the tangled tropic bower,
 Where the gay blossoms flaunt their scentless hues,
And parasitic tendrils, clinging close, refuse
To admit the sun-ray for a single hour:
Hide thee within the Saracenic Tower
That tops some Eastern hill, where ravens choose
Their croaking brood to rear, where clammy dews
Make sickly moisture for the fainting flower:
Hide thee within the Tomb: or seek the crowd
Where Fashion's empty votary lives and lies—
The dreary solitude of Creed and Caste :—
Thy heart still palpitates, thy head is bowed;
For a small voice within thy bosom cries,
' Be sure thy sin will find thee out at last.'

August 4, 1885.

A PHANTOM JUBILEE

A LEARNED man but lately drew a chart
    Whereon this Earth's great facts were all enrolled;·
Six thousand years this little sheet did hold;
A strange assemblage, both of truth and art,
In which the mightiest actors bore their part;
And all compressed within a single fold
Of paper, jostling one another, young and old,
And each contending in the world's great mart—
Empire, and lust of conquest, fame, remorse,
Murder and suicide and the poisoned bowl;—
Cleopatra and Elizabeth, strange to see,
Were side by side with Alexander's horse;
The wonders of all time, incongruous whole,
Were mixed to form this Phantom Jubilee.

FOREBODING

I KNOW not if the sufferings we expect
    Are lessened when they come, or if the pain
That sudden strikes us, when the heart and brain
No evil dream, no coming ill suspect,
Is worse to bear.   Rather, I think the first,
    For we so oft anticipate and dread
Some greater woe, when small ones come instead,
That our Foreboding is itself the worst.
The same holds good with Joy: we fondly hope
To realise our day-dream, eagerly look
For some fair vision far beyond the truth;
The soul o'erleaps its too contracted scope,
And treats its wish from some romantic book,
But finds, alas! its golden fancy—Ruth.

SYMPATHY

R ELIGION of the heart, in things Divine,
    Means love of God, and charity to men
In human matters; the Apostle's pen
Wrote words of fire, engraved upon the shrine
Within the holiest, 'Faith and Hope are nought
If Charity be wanting;' love to all—
Love, self-denying, calling nothing small,
Needing no learning though itself untaught—
From such there springs, as lesser springs from great,
Soft Sympathy, blue-eyed, with gentle voice,
Too generous e'en for friendship; all mankind
To her are friends, she owns none separate;
She has a heart for all, bids all rejoice;
One universal love fills all her mind.

1855.

EDUCATION

THE oak once lay within the acorn-cup;
  The infant holds the future of the man;
The minutes, fleeting, compass a life's span;
The raindrop swells the foaming torrents up;
Climate and soil make varied timber grow;
And differing educations change the child.
Time is resistless; terrible and wild,
In some dark seasons mountain-streamlets flow;
Thus Nature owns an outer influence,
But childhood most of all.   Be ours to guide
Their early days with the soft hand of love:
To teach the truth, and that with least pretence,
To show example none can e'er deride,
And point the way to happiness above!

1852.

·ADIEU

A FEW short days of pleasant intercourse,
    Of sweet communion of thought and soul,
Have passed away, as all things here must pass.
How few days pass and leave us quite heart-whole,
And as they found us! sorrow and remorse
Form the great retrospect of life, alas!
Yet these have sped, and memory survives,
To cast a 'longing, lingering look' behind;
For I might live a century of lives,
And never meet a Friend more true, more kind
Oh, think on me, as I shall ever dream
Of these bright hours of bygone happiness!
We glide in different barks adown life's stream.
I may not love thee more, I cannot less.

1855.

SONNETS

IN OTHER THAN ITALIAN FORM

HOPE ON—HOPE EVER

THE sun has mounted high ; the sickly drought
    Grasps the thin throat of many a fragrant flower,
And turns their lingering sweetness into death.
Poor life ! ephemeral, that sinks to nought
And dies, sad victim of a sunny hour,
Scorched in its childhood by a sultry breath !
Ah me ! how false are morning dews that raise
The promise of a bloom !   Sap rises free,
And green leaves sprout, and herald strength and life !
Thus have I seen the flattering dews of praise
Nourish the seed with hope and vigour rife,
And the hot glare of malice scorch the tree.
Yet Heaven's soft rain may quench the baleful heat ;
And some day Victory may atone Defeat.

THE DUEL

GREY, cold, and haggard rose the clouds that veiled
    The morning sun : e'en so the thoughts that paced
The narrow prison of his angry breast.

That stern, proud, anxious brow, too surely paled,
And through each swollen vein the hot blood raced ;
While dark resolve each throbbing pulse comprest.

To die is nothing : could he dare to kill
His fellow, and not pause ? Ah ! no : a smile
Lights up his face, as flowers adorn a tomb,

In every feature gleams determined will
That one must die. He reasons, ' Blackest guile
Calls loud for vengeance : 'tis a righteous doom.'

Then face to face—O God ! a moment more,
A flash, a cry, a fall, and all is o'er !

'SURTOUT SOIS JUSTE'

I WANDER in the body; but not less
   My wanderings take an insubstantial shape,
And in the hour when weary senses gape,
And vacant minds proclaim their emptiness,
My truant fancy travels far abroad;
And in grey twilight, as in golden morn,
'Mid joyous memories, 'mid thoughts forlorn,
She treads life's changing and precipitous road.
Help me, just Heaven ! to draw conclusions right,
Nor rashly blame, nor vainly praise too soon;
To stumble not in the dark paths of night,
Nor run too wildly in the full o' th' moon.
Thus young I prosper; and when bent with years
I cease to wander, thus gain kindly tears.

AN INTERIOR

A BLUE-VEINED marble, here and there besmeared
   With faded reddish stains, like blood long shed,
On forty pillars bore an oaken roof,
Worm-pierced and blackened, frowning grim and weird,
And graven with sad memories of the dead;
Eastward, a Moorish window, like a hoof
That narrows at the heel, let in the light
Caparisoned in colours; westward, shone
The brazen throats that swell the choir around,
Like spectral figures mystically bright.
Hark! soft and tender melts the dying tone,
Now full and clear—an avalanche of sound;
And now 'tis mute.   Ah! they who sleep below
Heed not the tide of music's ebb and flow!

E. R.

DIED 1851

HAVE all thy bright hopes faded? Has the night
 Of death victorious darkened o'er thy brow?

Are all thy dreams of life so soon decayed?

Are all thy thoughts of happiness laid low?

Yes! all are over, the too rapid flight

Of one brief year since thy fond vows were made!

Thy plighted troth, redeemed, has not yet passed,

And thou art gone, too bright, too pure to last!

Oh, cruel doom, in giving life to die!

Yet, happier fate, to leave some trace behind,

A relic of thy fair mortality,

Than all to perish in death's stormy wind!

Yet death's last boon is more than life can give—

For aye to rest, and yet for aye to live.

OXFORD: 1851.

TO A. A.

FOR twice eight days, dear Friend, from morn to eve,
    And after shades of eve have drawn to night,
And the full moon has silvered all the lake,
Lighting up glen and corrie with her light,
Have we, in vain, o'er Weather tried to grieve,
For each from other novel thoughts did take.
In fancy, I have trod grave Academe,
And thou, again, hast braved the purple tide
Where rolled in distant lands War's ruddy stream;
Or talked we not of some ideal bride?
To little purpose prayed we for the sun!
For ceaseless rain spoiled sport ere well begun;
Yet Friendship flourished, like a flame whose force
Is fed by tempests of opposing course.

    1855.

TRUTH v. PASSION IN POETRY

I WILL not own that 'Passion' is the food
 The Muse likes best to feed on; 'tis the life
Of much the wild and unrestrained desires
Of man find pleasure in; the true, the good,
The pure fair aliment of maid and wife
Is withered in those hot and sensual fires.
The Muse I love belongs to every age;
And, true herself, writes truth, and truth alone:
Nature and truth live pictured on her page;
Without the one the other were undone.
Thus the grey morning, half enwrapt in night,
Gives a cold welcome to the rosy light;
And thus the glowing sun, at evening's hour,
Takes half his beauty from a softened power.

1860.

L

TRUTH

WHO loves the Truth, and, clinging to his love,

    Lives for his love, and makes his love his life,

Detects in every lie the cruel strife

That shatters love, and casting down his glove

Becomes her Champion, nothing makes him quail!

He buckles her bright falchion to his side,

And grasps her lance, as some full-hearted bride

Grasps her new lord with love that cannot fail.

Oh! onward in that pilgrimage of power!

Forward! Enthusiast of the Truth, and live

In the deep love such life can only give,

Heedless of sunshine, or if storm-clouds lower.

Love, Truth, and Life in triple union stand

On Earth—in Heaven—an Eternal Band.

1852.

PHILOMEL

COME forth, and hear the Nightingale! the wind
    Scarce stirs a leaf; the moon has light enough
To guide our steps; in yonder wood I know
Where Philomel by night laments her mate.
The sky like armour gleams, sure sign of rough
Wild weather ere the morn: so trust the kind
And gentle evening that invites you now—
We prize God's simplest blessings all too late!
Hark! how each mourner strains a throbbing throat,
And triumphs in her ecstasy of woe!
Now the air rings with long-continued note,
And now the trembling cadence whispers low;
Faint Echo panting labours through the glade,
Such heavenly strains perplex the weary maid.

RAIN! RAIN!

FOR three-and-twenty days the purple head
    Of yonder mountain through the rain has frowned
Mist-clad, grey-glooming, weird, disheartening;
The swollen river overflows its bed;
Its waves, once bright, are dismally embrowned,
And the green valley weeps like living thing.
The deer, with drooping antlers, leave the crest,
And browse on soddened herbage at the base;
The grouse cower sadly, with bedraggled breast
And ruffled plumage, in some sheltered place.
All Nature longs for autumn's genial days
To shine once more beneath his ripening rays;
And I, with ready rifle, rod and gun,
Cooped idly here, am pining for the sun.

1855.

DEFENCE, NOT DEFIANCE

WE did not fly to arms in idle boast,
    To show fine stalwart forms in fancy dress,
To grasp a useless sabre, or to hold
A rifle for vain show, in emptiness.
We armed—still arm—to guard our sacred coast;
And in Defence the gentlest hearts grow bold.
Thus a free State free soldiers sends to fight,
'Aye ready!' and in earnest, when the vaunts
Of jealous neighbours overstep the right,
And eager preparation backs their taunts.
Then leap the youth of Britain from their rest,
And swear no stranger shall their homes molest;
E'en tenderest birds, provoked, grow brave in blood,
Beat back the invader, and defend their brood.

PURE LOVE

PURE Love is tender of another's pain,
　　Forgetful of her own; lives in the life
Another bears; forgiving, often weeps,
Yet never hopeless; counting loss for gain,
If that loss be but hers; averse to strife,
Though her keen watch o'er honour never sleeps.
Woe to pure Love whene'er her footsteps stray!
Woe to fond hearts when Passion fans the flame,
And brains distempered hold a hurtful sway,
And bandage up the eyes that guard her fame!
Then welcome death—sweet, tearless, sinless sleep,
Where slumber tempts not, and where eyes ne'er weep.
Far happier thus than when, Life's spring-tide gone,
Affrighted Reason flies her tottering throne!

A DAY IN JUNE

AND OTHER SONNETS OF NATURE

A DAY IN JUNE

A DAY in June! Not always bright and fair
Are English Junes; but this was given to me,
From all climatic imperfections free!
The South wind drove the sullen pulse of care
To distant North; and, glancing everywhere,
The frolic Sun made laughter; the young Tree,
Proud of his shadow and the courting Bee,
Held high his leafy front, to screen the glare!
The Hawthorn, in her bridal veil of white,
Shed a faint perfume o'er the peaceful scene;
The Thrush paused in his song to hear the Dove,
Who, late-imprisoned, floated like a Sprite
From bough to bough, and cooed amid the green
His plaintive pleading of monotonous love.

June 11, 1888.

THE WOOD-NYMPH

THE lime-trees shed their blossoms, and the scent
 Filled the light air that dallied round the grove;
The honeysuckle tendrils deftly wove
A net to catch them—sweets on sweets intent:
The thyme, scarce crushed (for She a-tiptoe went),
Breathed a faint tribute of its dying love,
Clinging about her footsteps as they move,
And all the wood in smiling homage bent.
Fair as young buds in early spring, one hand
Led in rose-fetters a new-captured fawn,
The other held a palm-leaf, from the stream
That trickled through the thicket—like the wand
Of some Enchantress. Gracious as the Dawn
She passed, this Oread of the Poet's dream.

October 13, 1878.

THE THROSTLE

I

THE throstle sang his loudest song to-day;

    Though the bleak North wind grasped his

        joyous throat,

It could not check the clear courageous note,

That welcomed March as cheerily as May.

'Tis surely wise to be thus early gay,

Nor wait for calms before we go afloat,

But bravely launch from shore our little boat,

And sing in hope our spring-tide Roundelay.

Such trust will be repaid; for they who wait

For summer, wait, and, fearing, wait in vain:

They who dare nothing, and restrain their song

Till the hour suits them, never can be great;

But will with troublous care and frequent pain

Make evil choice at last and take the wrong.

II

ALAS for confident philosophy!
    A few short hours, and all my braggart thrush
Can pipe to us is but a doleful 'Hush'—
'A white world' makes his hopes of spring to die,
And turns his love-song to despondency.
The snow hangs grimly on the lilac bush
Where yestermorn the leaflets strove to push
Through the thin sheaths where they imprisoned lie!
I would not therefore praise the over bold,
Who fall, as fell rash Phaeton from his car
By too much daring and too little art:
The earliest blossoms perish in the cold:
A skilful marksman shoots not over far:
Thus, midway steering, play we life's great part.

NATURE

THE heart contains the passions of the mind,
 The mind controls the passions of the heart:
So truth and feeling guide the painter's art,
And teach the ignorant to know their kind.
The poet revels in a fancied power,
Not his, nor yet another's, Nature's all;
His highest thought but answers to her call;
His noblest verses are her noblest dower;
Like poets, painters can create the life
That breathes upon their canvas, from a source
Unknown to many, yet true talent's force
Is Nature reproduced through patient strife;
Thus human art is humbled to discern
The God of Nature rules o'er all we learn.

1860.

WRITTEN FOR

ANGELA'S NATURAL HISTORY MAGAZINE

WHAT a dull World 'twould be, if only Man
 Were in it! Man the Tyrant! Man the Slave!
The vocal woods all silent as the grave,
And Nature cursed by some Almighty ban;
No swarm, ephemeral, that lives a span
Yet lasts for ever; the dark Ocean's wave,
No more aglow, from crest to inmost cave,
With fiery atoms, lustreless and wan!
Oh! what were life without a horse or hound—
(The Race, that makes the dullest pulse beat quick,
The Chase, that stirs the energies of Youth)—
Those dear companions of our daily round?
Oh! cherish them with love, tend them when sick,
And learn from them the honest ways of truth!

NIGHT

NIGHT—painted black-browed by the poet's pen,
  Gloomy, thick-veiled, at strife with honest deeds,
Star-studded, worshipped by a thousand creeds !—
·I greet thee well: welcome to weary men !
Not the sick souls who cavil at each day,
·Whose languid struggles imitate true work,
·Whose brawny shoulders honest labour shirk,
·And turn real·effort into idle play ;
But the keen hearts who resolutely strive,
From rose-crowned morning to the set of sun,
·To gain some end that knits the muscles close
(It may be merely pastime keeps alive
The strenuous exertion once begun)—
To these thou'rt welcome with thy glad repose.

THE RIVER

THERE is a River whose deep waters flow
    Silent and swift to a blue inland Sea;
And purple hills frown gloomily above,
And grassy meads smile tenderly below.
That River is the type of one whose plea
For many an erring word is Nature's love;
The ever-changing stream portrays his heart,
The purple mountains point at life's distress;
The meadows at the brink are fitting part
Of those who cheer him through this wilderness.
Yet blend the mountain, meadow, and the stream,
Then joys and sorrows in one band appear:
So, to my soul, dear friends, kind voices seem;—
With me they smile, with me they shed the tear.

1855.

TRANSLATIONS

M

FROM THE FRENCH

THE LEAF

'POOR withered leaf, canst say?
    Torn from thy stalk, dost know,
Where goest thou?'—'My stay,
    The giant oak, lies low,
Storm-smitten; from that day,
    All cruel winds that blow
Waft me alike astray,
    With their inconstant breath,
    In never-ending death.
Through forest, mountain, plain,
    Into the vale beneath,
    Where the winds guide, I go;
And yet I ne'er complain,
    Nor dread the doom of woe;
I share the common fate;
    The rose leaf and the bay
Must welcome the same state,
    And I must be as they.

FROM THE FRENCH

Victor Hugo

THE gracious God, whose tender mood
    Is known to those who pray and wait,
So thou art pure, and true, and good,
              Will bless thy fate.

The careless world that seeks to shine,
And sparkle with delusive flame,
So thou art fair, in cups of wine
              Will pledge thy name.

My heart, that in the loving light
Of thy dear eyes so fondly basks,
So thou art gay and glad to-night,
              No further asks.

FROM BÉRANGER

I

I 'VE laid more friends in sacred earth,
　Than danced for wedding or for birth :
I've often loving hearts relieved,
Who over self-made ills had grieved :
For this I thank God heartily.
For if nor wise nor strong am I,
I boast a mirth that ne'er offends
The deepest sorrows of my friends.

WRITTEN ON THE CATACOMBS AT ROME

FROM BÉRANGER

II

FROM the rich land, made fertile by thy power,
    Death lops the ears of corn.
Love, sweet restorer of the drooping flower,
    Cheers hearts too long forlorn.

E'en 'mid the crumbling ruins here around,
    We feel ' The Passionate Want.'
If Death thus reaps the harvest from the ground,
    Be ours the task to plant.

MY CONTEMPORARY

BÉRANGER

LOVE laughs to hear *you* boast the years,
    'Neath which, alas ! *I'm* doom'd to pine.
I wager that the Fates in tears
    Joined long ago your thread to mine.
These beldames then (so hazard brings
    Our fate) decreed as chance might be ;
You gained the summers and the springs,
    Autumns and winters fell to me.

THE BROKEN VIOLIN

BÉRANGER

COME, dear old dog, here, take thy share;
    Come, never notice my despair;
Eat; our last cake is sweet and good;
Black bread will be to-morrow's food.

Th' invaders cried yest're'en to me
(Though victors but by treachery),
'Play while we dance;' 'No, no,' I spoke;
So they my harmless fiddle broke.

It was our village orchestra:
No more gay feasts, no loud hurra
Will now be heard: who now can move
Young feet to dance, young hearts to love?

A lively measure played at dawn,
When the soft zephyr fanned the lawn,
Told to the maid who bent to hear,
The bridegroom and his train were near.

The reverend men, who heard the strain,
Ne'er deemed the jocund notes profane.
To see us smile, to hear us sing,
Had smoothed the forehead of a king.

If my poor fiddle now and then,
To the full voice of gallant men,
With patriot prelude, slumberers woke—
Was that a cause it should be broke?

Come, dear old dog, here, take thy share;
Come, never notice my despair;
Eat; our last cake is sweet and good;
Black bread will be to-morrow's food.

How slowly will the Sabbath pass
To idle lad and idler lass!
Can that sad vintage e'er be blest,
That sees my silent fiddle rest?

To weary ones we gave repose,
And lightened all the poor man's woes;
From great men, taxes, storms, and grief,
We only gave a sure relief.

We silenced many an enmity,
And brightened many a tearful eye;
No sceptre ever cheered the sick
As well as my poor fiddle-stick.

But as I turn to meet the foe,
I feel a patriot's courage glow;
And my sure musket, charged with lead,
Of broken fiddle stands instead.

If then I fall my friends will say
(Those friends with whom I may not stay):
'He would not play our well-loved strains,
For foes to dance on our remains.'

Come, dear old dog, here, take thy share;
Come, never notice my despair;
Eat; our last cake is sweet and good;
Black bread will be to-morrow's food.

FRAGMENT FROM BÉRANGER

YEARS will steal on thee, loved one; Time's dark wing
  Will shroud thy form when I shall cease to be.
Hours speed so quickly, memory seems to bring
  To my sad heart days doubly lost to me.
Live, live beyond my term ; but, oh ! let age
  Surprise thee, true, and tender of my fame ;
And in thy chimney-corner scan the page,
  And sing the verse that gives thy Poet fame.

When others seek in thy wan wrinkled brow
  The beauteous inspiration of my song,
And youth, that loves a tender tale, asks how
  He wont to woo thee, and why mourned so long,
Tell them, if words can tell, the amorous rage,
  The jealous rapture of my faithful heart ;
And in thy chimney-corner scan the page,
  And sing the verse in which thou bear'st thy part.

When they shall ask, 'Knew he the art to please?'
　'I loved him fondly,' needs no blush to say.
'Did he e'er vex, or e'er unkindly tease?'
　With tender pride your lips will answer, 'Nay.'
Then tell them, he could grief and pain assuage
　With touching music and the lute's soft tone :
And in thy chimney-corner scan the page,
　And sing the verse e'en when thy Poet's gone.

BÉRANGER'S LAST ODE

WHAT ! poor untutored children, dream ye still
    That Freedom is your watchword as of yore,
And that beneath her banner ye may fill
    Your cups to him who gave her life once more ?
Some foolish lays of mine in memory's heart
    Perchance survive ! forget them ! I would curse
My fame, if this the lesson they impart—
    Pardon the minstrel and his erring verse.

Where, where, to-day are the bright dreams complete
    I loved to hymn in all the flush of hope ?
I, who ne'er ceased to lash the race effete
    Of lacqueys, flatterers, Emperor, King, and Pope ?
'Tis true, I sang a mighty captain's fame,
    But, oh ! how fallen, crownless, and in chains ;
Brumaire recoils at St. Helena's name—
    Pardon the minstrel and his erring strains !

Must Nisard seem all-eloquent to be?
  Leverrier, too, a second Arago?
Are night's foul depths and silence dear to me?
  Can Belmontet e'er be to me Hugo?
And, oh! is my dear God of mercy One
  To whom the assassins and the gaolers pray?
Is Rome protected by His power alone?—
  Pardon the minstrel and his erring lay.

Yes! I have sung, in old heroic rhyme,
  The blue coats worn and torn in victory;
For they were the Republic's sons sublime,
  Who against banded monarchs learnt to die.
The dapper guard, who spies us as we pass,
  Who for promotion would his neighbour slay,
Is he my comrade drinking to his lass?—
  Pardon the minstrel and his erring lay.

To Poland and Italia's noble land
  France owes a debt—her blood; 'twill never flow;
Too near at home, on slippery ground we stand,
  The cannon booms—too late? 'tis madness now.

Go ! take your boasted freedom hence ; perchance
   The Turk may need such aid as yours ere long.
Ye nations, on your holy union glance.—
   Pardon the minstrel and his erring song.

FALLING STARS

BÉRANGER

SAY'ST thou, oh, Shepherd, that our star on high
Guides all our days, and glitters in the sky?
Oh, yes, my child ; but the dark veil of night
Hides the full splendour from our feeble sight.
  Thou read'st the secrets well, I ween,
  Oh, Shepherd, of that blue serene :
What star is that falls from the spheres,
And fades, and fades, and disappears?

My child, when at God's call a mortal dies,
His star shoots tremblingly athwart the skies.
That star, amid loved friends, whom happiness,
The grape's rich juice, and song, combined to bless,
  Near his dear wine-cup fell asleep;
  O'er such an end we cannot weep.
Again, a star falls from the spheres,
And fades, and fades, and disappears.

How clear, how pure, how beautifully bright!
Some charming being seeks the realms of light;
Blest in her home, and faithful in her love,
The tenderest heart is given to her above;
      Sweet flowers adorn the willing maid,
      And Hymen's altar stands arrayed.
Again, a star falls from the spheres,
And fades, and fades, and disappears.

That rapid star, that rushes from on high,
Was some proud prince of earth just born to die;
His cradle, emptied of its puny prize,
Was decked with gold and gems, and purple dyes,
      The poison of a flatterer's tongue
      Already in his ears had rung.
Again, a star falls from the spheres,
And fades, and fades, and disappears.

That lightning flash of dark ill-omened ray
Marked some official minion's dull decay,
Who deemed the mockery of others' pain,
Renown or place, or both perchance, might gain.
      The slaves who served a god so base
      Have hidden his portrait in disgrace.

N

Again, a star falls from the spheres,
And fades, and fades, and disappears.

Ah! weep, my son, from thy full heart, for yet
The loss of virtuous wealth may cause regret;
When the poor elsewhere gleaned a scanty hoard,
They reaped a goodly harvest at his board.
   There, e'en to-night secure of home,
   The indigent and needy come.
Again, a star falls from the spheres,
And fades, and fades, and disappears.

Some mighty monarch falls with it, be sure.
Go home, my son, and keep thy spirit pure;
And when thy star shoots its long lingering ray,
May neither wealth nor grandeur mark its way.
   If without doing good, tho' clear,
   Thou shin'st, at that dread hour thou'lt hear—
'Tis but a star that leaves the spheres,
And fades, and fades, and disappears.

FRAGMENT FROM THE FRENCH

Henri Murger

I

AS some sad relic of departed hours,
  And tender thoughts, to all save one, unknown,
A knot of riband, a few withered flowers,
  Shrouded in dust in some dark drawer is thrown ;

So have I flung aside the dead remains
  Of the first love that made my young heart beat ;
Their faded features ridicule the pains,
  And mock the vows, they can no more repeat.

Oh, days for ever fled ! whose halcyon beams
  Made the pale blossoms blush a deeper hue,
And brought reality to faintest dreams,
  That seemed too blissful ever to be true !

Oh nights ! dear nights, fit sequel to such days,
   Dear hours of night, whose every sigh was love ;
When silence on soft wing securely plays,
   And weeping Envy longs, but dares not move ;

When sleepless youth in feverish desire,
   Breathes the one name that lingers on his lips,
And drinks, drinks deep, voluptuous draughts of fire
   That scoffing age, alas ! now coldly sips !

Where are ye fled ? what sphere contains ye now ?
   The empty casket of my heart is left ;
But all the jewels that once decked the brow
   I loved so wildly, from the case are reft.

FROM THE FRENCH

HENRI MURGER

II

SINCE I have tasted of thy brimming bowl,
   And in thy hands have laid my aching brow;
Since I have breathed the incense of thy soul—
   Perfume, alas! for ever faded now—

Since, happy chance! thou heardst the tones that melt,
   Pour forth my loving heart's young mysteries;
Since I thy tears—thy sunny smiles—have felt
   Glow on my lips, and glisten in my eyes;

Since on my raptured head has dawned a beam
   From thy pure star—ah me! now veiled for aye;—
Since in the waters of my life's sad stream,
   A rose-leaf of thy morn has glided by;

Now say I boldly to each fleeting year,
   ' Pass on, pass ever, I defy thy power ;
Hence with thy flowers, all faded, worn, and sere ;
   Deep in my soul there blooms a deathless flower.

' Thy wing, so rudely balanced, cannot move
   One drop from my full cup of happiness ;
My soul still feels more fire—my heart more love
   Than thou hast ashes—or forgetfulness.'

FROM THE FRENCH

ALFRED DE MUSSET

WHEN first I loved thee it was joy to live;
    I loved thee more than all that life could give.
Yet I have ceased to love: well dost thou know
Who broke the promise, and who struck the blow.
Ah! all thy new-laid snares no more I fear,
In vain each smile, in vain each melting tear.
E'en as a child, who, of the dark afraid,
Creeps out of bed to seize some rusty blade;
Then, palpitating still, and scarce more bold,
Creeps back to bed, and trembles with the cold;
And when at early morn he wakes to find
His phantom nothing but a window-blind,
And sees his useless weapon all a sham,
Laughs and cries out, 'How great a babe I am!'

THE MUSE TO THE POET

ALFRED DE MUSSET

SING to me, for the wine of youth
  Fills all my veins with fire divine;
Sing to me, for the voice of truth
  .Is dead, and for thy voice I pine.

My bosom heaves, my lips breathe fire,
  Am I not fair enough to love?
Doth not each kiss invite desire,
  And charm thee to a world above?

Hast thou forgotten that first hour
  When, trembling at my quivering wing,
Thou yieldedst to the guiding power
  That now implores thee but to sing?

Then I requited all thy love ;
    Thou wast too fair, too young, to die ;
In pity sing, in pity prove,
    This night, how sweet is memory.

Oh ! sing to me, I still repeat ;
Where once I ruled, I now entreat ;
Hope bids me perish ; thou canst save
Thy slave—thy mistress—from the grave.

FROM LAMARTINE

AS in the pond that stagnates 'neath the wood,
  So in the soul are two things, bad and good ;
Heaven's azure, tingeing the dull sluggish green
With golden rays and tender clouds, is seen,
And the dark torpid pool that shuns the day,
Where reptiles creep their slimy life away.

REMEMBER

ALFRED DE MUSSET

REMEMBER when the morning ray
   Yields blushing to the god of day;
Remember when night, slow and pale,
Creeps beneath her silvery veil ;
When burning pleasure woos thy longing breast,
And lengthening shadows tempt thee to thy rest,
     List to the voice of love
     Echoing through the grove,
          Remember.

Remember when the hand of Fate
For aye decrees us separate ;
When years of woe have played their part,
And wither'd e'en my constant heart ;
Think then on me, and on my last adieu !
Time hath no power ! love rises fresh and new,
     And while my heart doth beat,
     Throbbing 'twill still repeat,
          Remember.

Remember in that hour of doom,
When cold I slumber in the tomb ;
Remember when the flow'rets wave
Gently, softly o'er my grave ;
I shall not see thee, but my soul divine
Will hold a sister-fellowship with thine.

　　In night's still hour, oh ! hear
　　My voice that whispers near,
　　　　Remember.

BEAUTY SLEEPING

LAMARTINE

HUSH! wake her not! cried he; but, oh! behold
    Those fairy features bathed in waves of gold;
That brow, where gentle peace and love unite,
And long dark lashes veil a skin so white;
That blooming cheek, whereon the chaste caress
E'en of a mother might half fear to press;
Those full ripe lips, parted by fragrant breath,
That just reveal the row of pearls beneath;
A throat more slender than the swan;—a line
Of figure full of harmony divine,
Soft as the ripple on the sleeping lake,
Ere the first breezes o'er its slumbers break;
Those rounded arms, that quickly heaving breast,
Which pictures love-dreams even in her rest;
And oh! those snowy archèd feet that bound,
And float in fabled fleetness o'er the ground,
Polished like pebbles on the ocean strand,
And still no larger than her mother's hand!

CHORUS OF THE CEDARS OF LEBANON

LAMARTINE

HOLY! Holy! Holy! Lord of the sacred mount!
   Beyond the starry realms His might we own;
As in the fragrant breath of night's full fount,
   We bend beneath His hand, as reeds bow down.
Why bend we thus?   'Tis that we bend in prayer;
   For a deep sense of heavenly virtue fills
   Each quivering branch, and all our foliage thrills,
     From deepest root to topmost head:
     As wrath that dyes his nostrils red,
     Like a fierce wind, swells in his breast,
     And drives the lion from his rest,
And on his neck raises the shaggy hair.
       Glide, glide, ye wandering breezes, by,
       And change to chords of symphony
       Each branch, each leaf, each fibred spray,
       That blossoms in the breath of day.

We are the sounding harp of Fame
That sings the God-endearèd name;
The moon-adorèd, dying, to live
For ever in the notes we give.
Blow, blow, ye gentle gales of night,
Down from heaven, up from earth,
In our branches, ever bright
With the name that gave you birth;
A thousand, thousand breezes blow,
Over the eternal snow;
If ye seek a herald's fame,
The lightnings will your power proclaim
By the sea, and by the sword,
By the unforgotten word!
And have we not a soul on high,
Whose every leaf sings harmony?

'GLORY to Thee,' eternal Sire!
Say what awful hand of fire
Thou layst upon the weakest moulds,
That our poor feeble fragile cone,
The foot of man might crush alone,
Such glorious forms as ours enfolds!

That from our tender fruit that lives,
And draws its being from the clay,
Should spring the mighty form that gives,
In leafy pillars, shade by day
Darker than clouds in murky flight,
To birds in thousands, rest by night!

What principle of life is there
In the rain-drop that we bear;
Of a sap, that at the first
A bird might drink, that still in size
In our veins it multiplies,
And of our vast fibres slakes the thirst?

That from this eternal fount,
In the lesser streamlets mount,
The torrent nothing can erase,
And from the crest, down to the root,
Makes green in turn, each branch, each shoot,
Like some vast hill, on pillared base.

Ye rocks! on whom our sure foundation rests,
Say on what day of days our roots were born!
Ye mountains! crownèd by our floating crests,
      Stars of the early morn,
      Of your young splendours shorn;

Meteors of night—seeds sown by his own power—
Say, if ye know, of our dread birth the hour?
Hard as the diamond are our trunks ; but there,
A thousand thousand years might be laid bare,
Writ in the veinèd fibres of our heart,
As elemental throes their stamp impart.

Heaven of night ! that hear'st our crested prayer,
Rocks ! to your inmost depths by us laid bare,
From whom a dewy nourishment we seek ;
Sun of the dazzling hair and golden cheek !
Ye nights ! who woo with kisses fresh and free,
And drops, like liquid pearls, each panting tree ;
     Say—for ye know—have we not sense,
     Sublime, acute, inspired, intense ?
Sense such as falls unto no other lot
In natural creation—Have we not ?
No lips, yet breathe we ; no eyes, yet behold,
Foretell, feel seasons, ere themselves unfold ;
Feed on the air, digest each floating breath,
Mysterious agents of life freed from death.

For whom are lotted ages of a life,
With soul, intelligence, and beauty rife ?

Is it for the dwarfling bush ?
The insect that a breath would crush ?
Or man, that phantom passing fleet,
Like withered grass beneath our feet,
Who deems this earth his throne, his home,
And vanishes ere from our dome
Our falling leaves have strewed his footprints o'er,
And in the light of day is seen no more ?
To-day, to-morrow's passing span,
'Tis thus we count the age of man !

YE eagles, soaring o'er our heads,
Go bid the winds unbind each chain ;
For, rooted in our rocky beds,
We bid defiance to their main.
Go ! bid these tyrants of the wave
Unfold their wings, and howl and rave,
And for the dire assault prepare ;
Bid them come on—their wildest shock
Our topmost shoots will hardly rock,
Or whistle through our waving hair.

Sons of the rock, self-born we stand,
Implanted by His holy hand ;

The diadem of green He shed
On sacred Eden's mountain head.
When earth is deluged by the wave,
Our hollow flanks His race will save ;
And children of the patriarch
From out our wood will hew the ark,
The chosen few who kiss the rod
Of aged Abraham's nomad God.

'Tis we who, when the captive band
View distant Hermon's promised steep,
Will spread our foliage o'er the land,
And o'er their shrines our vigil keep.
Or later, when The Word made Man,
By name more sacred calls His Sire,
Adorèd, ere the worlds began,
On the dread cross foredoom'd to expire ;
We are the altar raised on high,
Of sacrifice and agony ;
Ours the wood, for which atone   .
Nations at the Saviour's throne.

Men mindful of these prodigies,
Will bow their brows and shade their eyes,

And venerate each ancient mark,

And press their lips against our bark.

Saints, poets, sages far and near,

Voices in our leaves will hear,

Like mighty waters' falling sound

Echoing o'er the rocky ground,

And 'neath our old prophetic shade

Will utter hymns that ne'er shall fade,

But chime in music, as they sing,

With our own wild carolling.

GLIDE like a hand o'er the melodious lyre,

From chord to chord till ye at once inspire

To each a soul, and to each soul a voice!

Glide, ye night breezes, while our hearts rejoice;

And 'neath your touch each fibre of our frame

Will thrill with awe ecstatic at His name.

Let your long wings sweep through the arch'd recess

Of our old caves, and Heaven's own tear-drops bless!

The nightingale's soft murmur in her nest;

The ocean gently heaving in his rest;

The falling waters, bending grass;

The dewy saps, like rain, that pass;

The wild beast's moaning shrill-voiced roar ;—

Let Silence add her charms to make these more !

Each quivering herb, ay, every stone,

That earth prolific calls her own ;

Let them all raise a passionate cry,

Of one accord in harmony,

To Him in whom they live and die,

Their great Creator, who will deign to hear,

And succour all the feeble far and near.

Thou God ! Thou sea of infinite extent !

Thou fire divine ! of whom each life's a ray ;

Thou wondrous Whole ! in whom we all are blent ;

Thou who livest in endless day !

Immeasurable ! perfect ! and for aye !

Ever in spring-tide's hour of bloom,

Ere Nature was—beyond her doom—

Oh, let each sigh, that other days recall,

Rise up to Thee, Thou God, whence cometh all !

FROM THE FRENCH

Victor Hugo

    •

I N pity spare a fallen maid,
   Who knows beneath what wrongs she fell :
The pangs of famine undismayed
   Perchance she suffered—who can tell
What cruel storm did first uproot
And blast her virtue's tender shoot ?
For loving but too well—undone,
Her light of life for aye is gone.

Have we not seen poor tottering things
   Struggling in vain, all tired and worn,
E'en as a rain-drop fondly clings,
   And clasps the bough, altho' 'tis torn,
Till, trembler from its very birth,
Fair as a pearl, it falls to earth,
Where, reft of all its purity,
'Mid dust and mould 'tis doomed to lie ?

Oh! whose the blame? thine, cursèd gold,
  And ours who are thy ministers,
By whom these gems are bought and sold.
  He, who the wage of sin confers,
May blameless pass, unscorned, erect;
He mocks the crime that none detect;
But the poor victim of his lust,
A thing unnamed, must crouch in dust.

Yet e'en from out that dust the dew
  May shine in all its former sheen,
If but one sunbeam pure and new
  Should shed its radiance o'er the scene.
So may the fallen things of earth
Return to purity of birth;
So may love's sacred influence heal
The thousand pangs that women feel!

FROM THE RUSSIAN

NO time nor distance e'er can change
    The love I bear thee;
Nor separation e'er estrange,
    Nor sorrow tear me
From thee; for love like mine disdains
Terrors and tortures, grief, and pains;
    For loving once is loving ever,
    Past, present, future—faithless never!

Let hearts that cannot feel condemn,
    And all upbraid me;
Deride, accuse, reproach, contemn
    What thou hast made me.
They term it folly—be it so—
Raptures like mine they ne'er can know;
    For loving once is loving ever,
    Past, present, future—faithless never!

Let every accusation fall
    In thunder o'er me,
And dread misfortune's sable pall
    Hang black before me.
No angry threats can make me quail,
No menace force my love to fail;
    For loving once is loving ever,
    Past, present, future—faithless never!

FROM THE FRENCH

I LIKE to see the swallows,
  On quickly darting wing,
Bring each year to my window
  The promise of the spring!
The same soft nest will welcome
  The same old loves, they say:
'Tis only right such constant hearts
  Should have a sunny day.

And when the early snow-flakes
  Bring down the russet leaves,
The swallows call their kinsfolk
  From under the old eaves;
Fly, fly, from snow and north wind
  Let's haste away, they sing;
No winter for such constant hearts,
  Our season is the spring.

And if upon the journey
 It be some swallow's fate,
Caged by a cruel schoolboy,
 To be parted from her mate ;
Pining, but ever constant,
 From grief she fades away,
And her true love, hov'ring near her,
 Dies on the selfsame day.

FROM THE ITALIAN

I N the green morning-tide of day
   O'er the blue wave soft zephyrs play
And woo my spirit to repose,
And dry the tear that idly flows—
        For ah ! thou lov'st me not.

And when the brooding moonbeams take
An azure radiance from the lake ;
Like a bird tired of wandering,
The plaintive breezes ever sing—
        Alas ! thou lov'st me not.

I loved thee in my inmost soul,
E'en from the first I spurned control ;
And the dark garland of my grief
Bloomed, twined with many a rosy leaf—
        But ah ! thou lov'st me not.

Heaven gave to thee a sunny smile,
That lurked within thine eye, the while;
Thine envious lip seemed hardly glad,
But every word to me was sad—
        For ah ! thou lov'st me not.

Oh ! love me; when far, far away
I mourn in sorrow through the day;
And when at last to thee I fly,
Oh ! spurn my folly, bid me die—
        If thou wilt only love.

Ah ! let me love thee, and each care,
And joy, and sorrow, learn to share;
Let others woo the pomp of power,
And eager strive for honour's dower—
        Oh ! give me but thy love.

Hold up to obloquy my name,
Mock, scorn, upbraid, despise, defame;
Brand me with infamy, contemn,
Let all the world reprove, condemn—
        If thou wilt only love.

Then will my slowly winding doom
Glide gladly, quickly, to the tomb;
Then may my foes their weapons wield,
For each harsh word will be a shield—
　　　If thou wilt only love.

FROM THE ITALIAN

THE erring soul seeks a sad home in fate,
    When from her blest abode in Heaven she flies;
A passenger throughout this earthly state,
    A prisoner she weeps, and gasps, and dies.

In vain her sighs, in vain remorseful fears,
    In vain her fond aspirings for above,
In vain her birthright, and in vain her tears
    For Heaven—the everlasting fount of love.

Yet pitying Hope, clad in eternal rays,
    And meek Repentance lure the sinner on;
And from the mazy path, where Doubt still strays,
    Turns him to God, ere all his faith be gone.

FROM THE ITALIAN

PURER than the glittering spray
    That dews the petals of a flower;
Sweeter than the smiles that play
    O'er the lip in love's first hour;

Softer than the tender kiss
    From a mother's heart that leaps,
As she watches, in her bliss,
    O'er her firstborn as he sleeps;

Is th' affection ever flowing
    Thro' the spirit it imparts—
Breath of angels gently blowing
    Loving breezes o'er our hearts.

Dear one, full of this my breast
    Burns with essence all divine;
Kiss me, let the seal be prest;
    Friendship's sacred pledge is mine.

FROM ST. AUGUSTINE

E VER blooming roses redden in an everlasting spring;
O'er white lily, golden crocus, balsams dewy fragrance
    fling;

Pastures green, and corn-crops mellow, honeyed rivulets
    surround;

Breath of perfumed spices languish, aromatic balms
    abound;

From the never-fading branches, flowers in pendent clusters
    sway;

Neither moon nor sun, nor planet change the glory of their
    way,

In the ever-living lustre of the City of the Blest,

City of the Lamb Immaculate, where the weary are at rest.

HYMNS OF WAR

FROM AN ITALIAN TRANSLATION OF THE GREEK OF TYRTÆUS

HYMN I

Dulce et decorum est pro patria mori.—HORACE.

IN honour's cause 'tis fair to fall,
    For our dear land to give our breath
        With no regretful sigh;
With raging heart to challenge all,
And sword in hand, a soldier's death—
        'Tis God-like thus to die.

In such a fate the brave rejoice,
To such each hero's soul aspires,
        For such their fondest pray'r.
No wretched life of fear their choice,
Nor children blushing for their sires,
        And coward name they bear.

Who are yon crowd o'ercast with woe?
A spectre band, grim Famine's train,
      Without a kindly word
From those that hurry to and fro;
Each feature cramped by want and pain;
      Who tremble at a sword.

These are the men, without a name,
Who basely fled in danger's hour,
      Poor outcasts from their land.
Living, they forfeit honest fame;
And, dying, infamously cow'r
      Beneath opprobrium's brand.

Yet not alone their sires partake;
Their pale sad wives drink to the dregs
      The cup of dastard pain.
Their dying offspring cannot make
Their scoffs less bitter; pity begs
      A respite all in vain.

With drooping brows they hear each taunt
That dooms for aye the man they love
      In misery to roam ;
For he, who thus deserts each haunt
Of early youth, may ever rove
      And never find a home.

Oh ! let us banish pallid fear,
Bid trembling terror haste afar,
      Nor tempt our hearts to rest :
Here, in our inmost bosoms—here
They have no place, for burning war
      Inspires each generous breast.

Our country calls us to her side ;
Our children bid us wield the brand,
      And the fierce combat try.
Away, vain love of life—come pride !
If fair be victory, for our land
      'Tis fairer far to die.

Oh ! shame upon the coward throng,
Who leave their comrades in the fray,
      And fly themselves to save !
Their paltry life will not last long,
Their nearest kin will curse the day,
      And wish them in their grave.

Their very foes infuriate cry,
' Back, back, base slaves, to the vile earth
      From whence your natures came,
Unworthy of the death you die,
False to the land that gave you birth ;
      Dishonour to your name ! '

High, high they raise their matted hair,
Their blood-stained beards.   Oh ! agony
      Too horrible to tell !
Their trembling lips refuse the prayer ;
While curses, ringing loud and high,
      Are the coward's funeral knell.

What brow but reddens 'neath the shame?
What hoary sire but lifts his voice
               In deep and stern reproof?
An early death had saved their fame;
For, honour safe, all hearts rejoice;
               When lost, all stand aloof.

For brave men never die; their praise
Still leaps exulting from the grave,
               And mocks its vaunted power.
And tender maidens chant their lays
By moonlit hours, and woo the brave
               With many a fragrant flower.

HYMN II

Let the gods so speed me, as I love the name of honour more than I fear death. —JULIUS CÆSAR.

H E who hears the war trump sounding,
    Fiercely gazing on the foe,
All his soul with frenzy bounding—
    He the joy of fame shall know.

He alone can claim true glory,
    He alone is really brave,
Who in battle, grimed and gory,
    Bids defiance to the grave.

Slander flies away before him;
    Praises echo in his ears;
Deathless glory hovers o'er him,
    And posterity reveres.

Mighty nations homage render,
  In the hero all delight;
His dear country's best defender,
  Ever foremost in the fight.

Fear he knows not, flight despising,
  Bold his heart, and firm his eye;
His soul above all danger rising,
  Deems it God-like thus to die.

None are near him, still he gazes
  Fiercely on the bloody surge;
Still his piercing voice he raises,
  Still he plies his deadly scourge.

Then he falls, the sisters hoary
  Cut, at last, the fatal thread;
But the wide wound marks the glory
  And the lustre of the dead.

Stark he lies, his helmet broken;
  Pierced his breast, his mail beneath;
But he grasps his sword in token
  Of a faithful friend in death.

Men and maids with bitter anguish
   Mourn the hero ta'en away;
Aged bosoms droop and languish
   For the mighty gone for aye.

On the bier in many a cluster
   Laurels yield a sacred wreath;
All who knew him, weeping muster
   Round the sad abode of death.

A few stones his sole dominion;
   A little earth is all he needs;
Fame uplifts on deathless pinion
   Record of his glorious deeds.

E'en the children that come after,
   Think upon his fame with pride;
Whisp'ring, as they hush their laughter,
   ' He to save his country died!'

Noble youths applauding vaunted
   Of the valour of their Lord,
Of the mighty spoils, undaunted,
   That he purchased by his sword.

Aged warriors, bent and hoary,
 Cry, half weeping in their joy—
' Blessèd be thou, son of glory !
 Be thou like him, oh, my boy ! '

Thus, whoever proud and peerless
 Claimeth glory as his right,
Let him hasten, firm and fearless,
 To the thickest of the fight.

HYMN III

To triumph and to die are mine.—GRAY'S *Bard.*
Cowards die many times before their death.—SHAKESPEARE.

OH! mighty offspring of a mighty sire!
 Swell not your valiant hearts with warlike fire?
Doth not the war trump wake ye? far and near
The mocking laugh resounds; away with fear!
Hand to the sword! 'tis but a passing cloud
That veiled your valour from the eager crowd.
Hand to the sword! curs'd be the craven slave
That fears the foe, or dares not face the grave.
Sons of the brave, yourselves as brave, arise!
Recall to memory your sires' emprise;
They taught not how to fly from death or pain,
Not e'en when slaughter strewed the reeking plain.
They little recked, altho' the day were lost;
Each man, a hero, battled with a host,
And prayed that he might perish in the strife,
For death was better than a coward's life.

Ye know how fair the hymn of praise resounds,
How sweet an ointment to a soldier's wounds.
Ye know how dark th' abyss, the gulf how great,
Between the hero's and the coward's fate.
Ye heard the bitter scoff that jeered the flight
Of foeman routed in the deadly fight.
Ye saw the dastard feet, so swift to fly,
Shackled with iron in captivity.
Thrice happy he, who, foremost in the strife,
Gluts his keen blade with many a hostile life;
Who cares not for himself, whose only cry
That thrills each heart is, Death, or Victory !
Yet he who meets Death's menace with a smile
Will oftener from his prey the tyrant wile,
Than the pale wretch who, crouching from his face,
Brands his own honour with the dire disgrace:
O'erthrown the coward lies, his quivering form
Like the reed shattered by the raging storm ;
And his last dying notes of terror speak
In dank and blood-grimed hair and pallid cheek.
No stifled sob can choke the rising breath
Of wife or brother at his dastard death;
And the deep wound, that gashed him as he fled,
Will bid them blush for the dishonoured dead.

The noble warrior, burning in his rage,
Burns for the fame that lives in history's page;
Gnaws the full lip, and rushing to the fray,
Defies the perils that attend the way.
From those he loves he listens to the fame
That sounds the God-like glory of his name.
The aged father whispers to his boy,
' Be thou like him, and thou wilt make my joy.
Up for the fray ! gird on thy trusty steel ;
Where the fight rages with the fiercest zeal,
Charge on ! cleave down ! strike home thy thirsty brand
Till sinking nature bids thee stay thy hand.
In serried phalanx each to each draws nigh,
Breast joined to breast, in valiant sympathy ;
Foot pressing foot—that surer be thy stand
Where'er thou battlest for thy native land.
Buckler to buckler, as befits the brave ;
Helmet to helmet, powerful to save ;
Go where war's tempest rages darkest—there,
There thou mayst slay and riot free from care.'

STANZAS FOR MUSIC

SING ON

SING on, sing on, I cannot tire
　　To hear thy loving voice ;
Thy strains, that breathe a chasten'd fire,
　　Bid my sad heart rejoice.
Sing on, sing on, I love to hear
　　The melody repeat
The hopes of youth, without a fear
　　That time speeds on too fleet.

Sing on, sing on, and as thy notes
　　Throb on my soul's dull chord,
Another boyhood fondly floats
　　Around me at each word.
Sing on, sing on, 'twere needless pain
　　To stay the illusive tone,
Or break the charm that speaks again
　　Of joys long past and gone.

Yet no ! I would not have thee bring
   Too vividly to me
The loved ! the lost !   Forbear to sing,
   Or change the melody.
Ah ! change it, and bid Love's sweet strain
   Its magic o'er us fling,
And bind us with its golden chain.
   Sing on, dear minstrel, sing !

REUNION

I

OH ! what is there in this world so sweet
  As a kiss when lips, long parted, meet;
The tender answer of loving eyes
To words unasked in the glad surprise
Of a longed-for meeting—unlooked-for joy—
Which all Time's skill can ne'er destroy—
The sudden spasm—delicious pain—
When lips, long severed, meet again?

II

I do not sing of effeminate bliss,
The moist return of the daily kiss;
But when years pass, and Oceans part,
And faith is firm—the kiss of the heart.

The vanished doubts, the trusting smiles,
The welcome glance that care beguiles;
The pressing palm, and—who can tell?—
The far-off sound of a Wedding Bell?

January 14, 1888.

CONSTANCY

'HE comes! He comes!' she softly cried;

   'He comes!' the wanton birds replied;

The wayward breeze in silence sighed;

The twilight flushed—then slowly died.

.   .   .   .   .   .

But soon her hopes—so fond, so high—

Faded like childhood's memory.

.   .   .   .   .

The parting swallows pitying cry,

   'Come with us to a kinder sky;'

But the lone watcher made reply,

   'Had I dove's wings I would not fly,

But wait and wait until I die.'

    March 28, 1885.

'THE SILVER SONG'

A. A. P.

'THE silver song,' ay, sing it, little bird !
  Borne thro' the realms of air
Till echo, by thy tuneful treble stirred,
  Repeat thy tender pray'r.
Bid all thy playmates in the forest raise
  Their blended notes above,
A glorious choral hymn of grateful praise,
  A symphony of love
Through the dark aisles, where Nature's builders plant
  Her arches on the sod,
A grand cathedral, where a full choir chant
  Their psalmody to God !

REMEMBRANCE

Nessun maggior dolore
Che ricordarsi del tempo felice
Nella miseria.   DANTE.

OH ! let them flow, I love each trembling tear—
    Sad solace to a heart that still bleeds fast ;
Ah ! dry them not, but let my eyelids wear
    The veil that shrouds the past.

Why say'st thou, Dante, that in hours of woe
    A joyous memory is the worst of grief?
What anguish made such bitter words to flow ?
    Has sorrow no relief?

Must we forget the Morning's cheering rays,
    Because the Night her sable vesture brings ?
Ah ! no : true pleasure lives in other days,
    Remembering happier things.

BIRTHDAY RHYME

I LAY no offering on the shrine
   Where suppliants kneel and captives pine ;
But all a wandering minstrel brings
Are his poor harp's untutored strings.

The happy day that saw thy birth
(Each year renewed with festive mirth)
Smiles on thy charms, that Nature made
So faultless they can never fade.

No virgin-gold can shine more fair
Than the bright ripples of thy hair ;
No ocean pearl, no flake of snow
Be whiter than thy queenly brow.

Then, lady, trust not gold nor gem,
Rich coronet nor diadem ;
True beauty flashes from those eyes,
That tinselled baubles can despise.

But, oh ! on this thy natal day,
Accept the homage that I pay ;
And take my verse in kindly part,
And trust the bard, though poor his art.

MEMORY

HOPES of the past ! ye rise before me
  As incense from the censer springs ;
A perfumed cloud, ye hover o'er me,
  And to the shadow memory clings.

Intangible, yet penetrating
  The inmost soul with joy or pain,
Ye float, my senses captivating,
  So far, so near, and all in vain.

I bid you welcome, for I love you
  And yet your near approach I dread ;
The present has no power to move you,
  Ye live for ever, although dead.

What will the future bring?   I wonder,
  For as I write fleet time has past ;
Clothe it in zephyr or in thunder,
  One thing I know—it cannot last.

And when grief comes, as come it may,
  Time still inflexibly rolls on;
To-day glides into 'yesterday;'
  The brightest, like a dream, is gone.

Yet have we left (as rose leaves faded
  Live in the bowl, in death more sweet)
Hopes of the past, by time unshaded,
  Which memory fondly may repeat.

THE HALF-OPENED ROSE

I AM old, but I love the soft perfumes of youth,
  Which in mead, or in garden, glad Nature bestows ;
And the scent I love best, sweet as love, pure as truth,
  Is the fragrance that breathes from a half-opened rose.

There are myrtles and jasmines that cling to young brides;
  I am old, and I care not for weddings and cake ;
And orange flowers luscious, and others besides ;
  But my own sweetest rose I will never forsake.

I am old, and ere long the dark curtain must fall
  On the scene where I've played out the drama of life ;
And my couch for its hangings must take the dark pall,
  When I sigh a sad farewell to children and wife.

Then dress me no wreath of immortals, nor weave
  A garland of cypress to cloud my repose ;
But when my last friend takes a sorrowful leave,
  Let him lay on my bosom a half-opened rose.

SONGS OF BIRDS

I CARE not what the blackbirds say,
  I heed not what the mavis sings,
When, poising on the rowan-spray,
  Their voice through all the woodland rings.

But dull the heart, and poor the brain,
  Or else enwrapt in thought intense,
Or saddened with o'erwhelming pain,
  That fails to catch the jocund sense.

To them the sun shines warm and bright,
  They feel the joy of azure skies;
The early morning's rosiest light
  Makes prelude for their melodies.

They warble from the sunny banks,
  They whistle from the golden braes;
And each small songster hymns his thanks,
  And strains his throat with grateful lays.

When poppies blush, and blue-flowers smile,
  And busy reapers stook the grain,
And valleys 'laugh and sing' the while,
  Their notes make music o'er the plain.

So lift thy voice, glad heart! in praise,
  For blessings garnered at their prime,
And to thy God thanksgivings raise,
  Like little birds at harvest time.

LOVING FACES

H OW the smile of loving faces,
    And the thoughts of days gone by,
Tender words, and well-known places,
    Fill the founts of memory !

Kindly greetings, gently spoken
    By old friends, with hope are rife ;
And clasp'd hands, dear simple token,
    Call dead feelings back to life.

Time may sunder, years may sever,
    But, like swallow to his nest,
Oh ! my faithful heart flies ever
    Homeward for a place of rest,

Where the warmth of pure affection
    Brightens every painful toil,
Lightens labour, cheers dejection,
    Even on an alien soil.

WHAT MATTERS IT
WHEN THE END IS SURE?

That matters not ; let come what will ; at last the end is sure ;
And every heart that loves with truth is equal to endure.

TENNYSON.

I

OH ! what can it matter, if Love be sure?
    For hearts that are true can learn to endure,
Endure through the struggles and pains of Life
If the end be certain—Husband and Wife!

II

Oh ! what can it matter though Time be slow
And the raven curls are powdered with snow?
For Hope sustains us and Patience bears
With a smile and a sigh our passing cares.

III

Oh! what can it matter, a year or more?
Our barks are nearing the selfsame shore ;
Though adverse winds may our course delay,
We are clear in sight of the welcome Bay.

IV

But woe to the Lovers when doubts arise,
And they scan the gloom of their leaden skies—
The smallest syllable makes them rue,
And breaks the hearts that were once so true.

April 16, 1888.

INSOMNIA

AND OTHER MISCELLANEOUS POEMS

INSOMNIA

THROUGH all the weary night I lay,
   It seemed a century or more,
   A ship that struggled for the shore,
Yet came no nearer than the bay.

For hours and hours I fondly gazed
   Athwart the Eastern window-pane ;
   For hours and hours I looked in vain
To where the great Aurora blazed.

I faint with longing for the morn,
   Oh ! leaden hours that creep and creep ;
   Oh ! cruel thoughts that murder sleep,
And shake my faith and rouse my scorn.

Haste on your Pilgrimage of Woe,
   And waste your spite on me no more ;
   I see the chink beneath the door
Begins to glimmer and to glow.

Oh ! welcome light to sleepless eyes,
   The first pale glint of yellow day,
   That peeps with hesitating ray,
And fills me with a chill surprise.

The restless limbs, the weary head,
   May seek the solace of the sun,
   May walk, may climb, may leap, may run,
Untrammelled by their hated bed.

I hear the jalousies thrown back,
   The muffled sound—the tremulous tread—
   And, like one listening from the dead,
I hear the polished parquet crack.

And up I spring with might and main,
   And cast the cerements all aside,
   The pillows falling far and wide ;
And now I am alive again.

OUR ONE SALVATION

OH CHRIST ! with clay Divine anoint mine eyes
    That I may see Thy truth ; bid my lame heart
Leap up with hallelujahs to the skies,
And in Thy Heritage, Jesu, give me part.

Lord, I believe, help Thou mine unbelief.
I totter, tremble ; Thou alone canst save,
And to my sufferings bring a sure relief.
Where is thy Victory, Death? thy Sting, O Grave?

Yet ere I pass for ever from this world,
Where Love can conquer Sin, and Grief, and Hate,
Accept my pain for that of others, hurled
To outer depths by ignorance and fate.

Grant, gracious God, this expiation now,
Not for myself—for am I not forgiven?—
That others too may see their sins as snow,
Though Conscience tells their souls are justly riven.

Drive dark Despair, and all the fiends that cling
To sinful man, back to their own damnation ;
Teach them to trust in Jesus, and to sing
His one Redemption and their own Salvation.

TO MAKE DEATH A GAIN

TO live in vain ! self-seeking, and content
    To rise on others' ruin, nor repent
When the dark Angel's wings are round him spread,
And, save some feeble pulses, he is dead.
This is to live in vain ! The kindest eye
For such a life—save Pity weeps—is dry.
No warning voice such erring soul can save,
No weeping friends surround the loveless grave.
But when the stroke of Death attacks the Just—
And to the best and wisest come it must—
Perchance a moment's warning, and no more,
Ere the long voyage to the unknown shore :
No matter, for a smile of holy peace
Illumes the dying saint, whose troubles cease ;
His vast possessions give him no more care,
They pass to others, to a weeping Heir.
His honest life secures a happy end,
And all who knew him mourn the generous friend.

He only grieves not, but resigns his breath
To God who gave it, cheerful e'en in death.
Content to live, if God should so decree;
Content to die, if so His will should be.
This is to live, and not to live in vain;
This is to die, and to make death a gain!

FAR FROM HOME

A S cagèd birds, in the dark hours of night,
 Feel the wild longings of a rapturous flight,
Soar in the spirit o'er the topmost trees,
Float fondly buoyant on the tropic breeze,
Cross the wide ocean, stem the tempest's force,
Yet keep unswerving to their destined course,
Escape a thousand perils, till they come
Nearer and nearer to their long-lost home ;
Already straining all their tiny quills,
They half forget their tortures and their ills ;
Already chirping their familiar cry,
They listen, longing for the loved reply ;
Already chosen is their place of rest,
Already built their cunning hidden nest,
Already Fancy with too sanguine mood
Supplies the nest with all its callow brood ;
Already reared, they learn short flights to wing,
And taught by love their little song to sing ;

When some rough hand too rudely breaks the spell,
Turns Fancy's Heaven to a Captive's Hell,
Dispels each hope and wakes them from a dream
Of happy days that are not what they seem,
Dooms them in man's rough custody to lie,
Their best, their only, happiness to die;
Or the bright advent of imperious day
Wakes the poor dreamers with intrusive ray,
Dispels their visions with the fading stars,
And leaves them fluttering 'gainst their prison bars :
So have I known, by some far distant stream
Some hapless exile, wakened from his dream,
Where golden Ganges with its freight of souls,
Or some remoter wave, its water rolls,
Where the hoarse dingo bays the moon at nights,
Or weird Aurora sheds her Northern Lights,
Where lions guard the fountain's narrow brink
And timid antelopes scarce dare to drink,
Alike in Asia or in Afric's land,
By icebound coast or some too torrid strand,
Wherever Ocean earth to earth unites,
Or fair Adventure youth and health invites ;
There far from home some cagèd mind will pray,
In those still hours that bound the lightsome day,

In the faint accents of his boyhood's glee,

Learnt at the altar of his mother's knee,

For the dear home he wantonly resigned,

The parents, sisters, friends, he left behind ;

And it may be will picture o'er and o'er

The well-known haunts, the once familiar shore,

The paths he trod through many a fernclad glade,

The tender glances of some blue-eyed maid,

The happy ploughboy and his dappled team ;

A thousand childish thoughts will crowd his dream,

A thousand hopes, remembered but too well,

In that sad hour his aching heart will swell,

Till, wearied out, he bids them all be still,

Nor sweet nor sorrowful his bosom fill ;

For well he knows the hour of waking near,

And from his eye there falls one human tear,

One tear, that tells how much remains of good

In all the wreck—in that still wayward mood,

That through the changes of his dark career,

In nights of revelry, in days of fear,

The tender teachings were not all in vain,

They lightened sorrow and they softened pain ;

And if not always, yet at times were heard,

Like the soft echoes of the dreaming bird,

The still small voice that, far above the din
Of riotous laughter or of graver sin,
Pierced with a sure remorse the erring heart
And turned it longing for the better part,
Longing to break the prison bars and fly
Far from the noisome cage to some pure sky,
Where childhood's innocence and childhood's play
Would hide the past, drive memory away,
And in the present find a new-won joy,
The love of all he loved when still a boy.
Then can he see, with something like surprise,
What erst was hidden from his blinded eyes,
The honest love that said its simple say,
Fearless of scandal, unabashed by day,
As our first parents, guileless ere the tongue
Of lying serpent tempted Eve to wrong;
Such God-inspirèd passion fills the heart
Of all created nature, 'tis a part
Of Nature's self—in shrubs, in herbs, it lies—
And wanting this our very Nature dies.
In the gaunt desert where the Palm-trees draw
A poor exotic life, 'tis Nature's law;
In the thick forest where the Lions rove
And birds in thousands sing—their note is love.

The swinging parasites embrace the trees,
They, fondly sighing, woo the summer breeze ;
While at their feet cryptogamous unfold
Myriads of ferns in silver, green, and gold ;
Each vies with each in lusty nature fair
To reproduce its kind, its loss repair :
Each wars with sad destruction's fetid breath,
And grapples grandly with the grasp of death.

TOO LATE

AN EVERYDAY ROMANCE

WHICH shall it be, Love, which shall it be,
    Strife with him, or peace with me?
Which is the brightest, which is the best,
A hateful struggle, or loving rest?

What can the world and its minions say
Worse than the words you have heard to-day?
False they may be, and black of hue,
But you know in your heart you wish them true.

Which shall it be, Love, which shall it be,
Tears with him, or smiles with me?
November frost or an April sky,
When the Summer's light wing is hovering nigh?

Be brave, and choose—nor think of the world
With its careless comments at random hurled—

But please yourself—and I know *my* fate,
And *yours*, poor Child, if you hesitate.

Which shall it be, Love, which shall it be,
Despair with him, or hope with me?
Hope, in some fairer clime, to find
A joyous home and a kindred mind.

Hope, to forget on some southern shore,
The doubts that shall never trouble you more.
Which shall it be, Love, which shall it be,
Death with him, or life with me?

.   .   .   .

He paused—and she slowly rose—but turned
One pleading glance—one look that burned
Like a fiery flash—on the suppliant face,
Whose longing eyes were a mute embrace.

Then, in a tender voice, she cried—
'Would I had died, Love, would I had died,
Ere from thy lips I had heard my fate,
Only to answer—Too Late, Too Late!'

Tears, great tears from her sorrowful eyes,
Tears, like the rain from Summer skies,
Dropped through the fingers that hid her face,
And fell on the folds of her bridal lace.

Yet once again she looked up, and spake—
'It may be, belovèd, some dire mistake,
Some cruel error has rent my heart;
But the hour has passed for regrets—we part—

'I to a hated but promised life—
A broken-hearted and loveless wife—
And you, perchance, to a truer troth,
May God in His mercy sustain us both!'

.   .   .   .   .   .

Never, I swear, till my days be past;
Never, Love, never, while life doth last,
Shall my lips by another's lips be stained,
Or my love by another be profaned:

If thou wilt leave me, Oh heart of stone!
Thou leavest me now, and for ever, alone—
Alone—as a bird in captivity—
Alone to live—and alone to die!

Farewell, I bless thee : I cannot curse,
For thy bitterest foe could not wish thee worse,
Joyless and childless with him to dwell,
Pitiful, pitiless, oh, farewell !

.   .   .   .   .   .

The Rowan is red in the old churchyard,
The leaves by the breath of Winter are scarred,
And a plain headstone with a name and a date
Has for Epitaph only—'Too Late, Too Late !'

January 10, 1888.

HADRIAN'S ADDRESS TO HIS SOUL

ANIMULA! vagula, blandula,
    Hospes comesque corporis,
Quæ nunc abibis in loca—
Pallidula, rigida, nudula,
Nec, ut soles, dabis jocos?

TRANSLATION.

Oh! tender Soul without a home,
Dear Guest and Comrade of this clay,
Now that thou may'st no longer stay,
Where wilt thou go? or whither roam—
Pale, naked, grave, and well-nigh dead,
All thy accustomed humour fled?

March 9, 1885.

TO GORDON

OH !. guileless warrior, though thy mortal frame
    Rest with the swarthy foes thou lov'dst too well,
To the whole world belongs thy martyred name ;
    But here thy spirit must for ever dwell.

1885.

AN EPITAPH

THEY mourn who knew him not; how then
    Must they who knew him weep ! The fate
Of all is death; and wisest men
Reflect that they—or soon or late—
Must draw the lot, and so prepare
Their lives, in love and labour spent;
Not unrewarded if they share
Our sorrow. Thus he calmly went
To join the great ones gone before,
And thus we weep; a theme for all !
God guide him to that friendly shore
Where tears are dried before they fall !

JOHN BROWN

A LOWLY subject and a mighty Queen—
    How great the social gulf that lies between !
Can worth, fidelity, and truth do more
Than try to span it?   Yes—can bridge it o'er !
And cruel Death that lays the subject low
From Royal eyes makes kindly tears to flow,
And with a sorrowing heart these words to own,
' Here lies my true and faithful friend, John Brown.'

A STRAY THOUGHT

FOR sacrifices we have made
    We're oft unconsciously repaid,
If not by human hands, by One
Who knows far better why they're done,
And sends us sorrow, grief, and pain
To be at last our priceless gain.

THE BLIND MAN'S PRAYER

FATHER of light, God of the glorious day,
    And starry wonders of the skies,
To Thee I raise my voice, to Thee I pray,
    And lift my sightless eyes.

The azure heaven, illimitable sea,
    The forest giants' leafy screen,
Are all a dead, dull blank of space to me,
    And never to be seen.

For me no flowers unfold their countless hues,
    For me no verdure decks the plain;
The sun's meridian rays the light refuse,
    For which my eyeballs strain.

The passionate stream that pours from eyes that love,
    The tender glance affection gives,
The lustrous smile from lips that mutely move
    In eloquence that lives,

Are lost for me ; the blind man's senseless stare,
　Alas ! falls dimly, darkly dead,
Void, viewless, vacant as the empty air
　That fans my fevered head.

The fair proportions of Thy solemn fanes,
　Whose aisles expanding arches grace ;
The sculptured beauties, and the gorgeous panes
　That holy pictures trace,

Unseen by me, make not my spirit feel
　Purer in prayer—more truly Thine !
As dumb men voiceless pray, I sightless kneel
　To worship at Thy shrine.

IN MEMORIAM

DECEMBER 14, 1861

I HEARD a sound by night that chilled my blood,
    And smote upon each sense ;
And as I hurried by, I sudden stood
    In listening most intense.

I knew, when monarchs threw their Purple down
    At Death's supreme appeal,
The great Cathedral bell tolled o'er the town,
    A tone the dullest feel.

Did I now hear that unexpected note
    Of sorrow and of death,
Borne through the city from an iron throat,
    With slow convulsive breath ?

Or fancy-heightened, did some jangling chime
    From parish steeple, feign
That knell of Princes, only knoll'd what time
    The highest cease to reign ?

Alas! too surely Death had 'swum the foss,'
    And 'pierced the castle wall;'
And the full echo swells a nation's loss,
    And spreads our Prince's pall.

An English Prince in everything save blood,
    The Consort of our Queen,
Had perished in his prime; the Wise, the Good,
    Was only what *had* been.

No haughty planner he of lawless law;
    No meddler in the State;
With clearer eyes than other men, he saw
    How Princes should be great.

Where meek-eyed Art and strong-armed Science dwelt,
    He loved to tarry near;
And in those virtues less perceived than felt,
    He was without compeer.

No Court intriguer he; none ever proved
    More loyal to his wife;
No father showed the children whom he loved,
    A purer rule of life.

He saw our weakness, and he made us strong ;
  Our trials shared, and knew
The world's applause to be an idle song,
  Which every zephyr blew.

In the straight path of rectitude he trod,
  Guide, counsellor, and friend
To that dear Lady, to whose grief may God
  Sure consolation send !

F. B.

In Memoriam

ANGEL! that guardest her pure heart,
　　Unfold thy wings, for she is thine,
　　And now her spirit, all divine,
In earthly troubles has no part.

Bear her on high to that blest sphere
　　Where Christ's own chosen wait the end;
　　And heavenly consolation send
To those who sorrowing tarry here.

Nor yet delay; from God's own throne
　　Waft down thy balm from healing wings,
　　Where the bright seraph ever sings
Soft hymns of comfort to the lone.

Weary and lone, indeed, are we,
 And, blind with tears, in darkness grope;
 Yet mourn we not without our hope,
For young and aged turn to Thee.

We feel—we know—that she is there,
 To guard and guide us as of old;
 Her tender presence makes us bold,
We joy to know her freed from care.

We feel, we know that she is near,
 Her spirit hovereth around;
 Among the pure still purest found,
Her memory sanctifies us here.

MY FIRST-BORN

THE baby, from his birth, was weak,
    Had he died sooner, she had sooner died;
The first faint words I heard her speak
    Were—'Love! our boy lives! lay him by my side.'

How long he lived I scarcely know,
    But ah! she spoke the cruel, cruel truth;
I laid them side by side, and now
    Life has no love for me, and all is ruth.

ARTHUR WELLESLEY,
DUKE OF WELLINGTON

THE Hero chief has fallen. The night
    Of death has quenched the beacon light ;
With lowly head and drooping crest,
He slumbers in eternal rest.

When danger darkened every ray
That cheered the noon-tide of his day,
When human prowess seemed too late
To save the realm, avert the Fate,

The rapid glance of his stern eye
Seemed every danger to defy,
Seemed every terror to abate,
To nourish Hope, and scoff at Fate.

T

Yes ! all unmoved in peril's hour,
Did changing Fortune smile or lower :
He heeded not—as one who threw
A deeper stake than mortals knew.

In war, in council, in debate,
The first, the best, to guide the State ;
He triumphed wheresoe'er he trod ;
Nor bowed the knee, except to God.

At last the Hero, stern in fight
(Of senators the beacon light) ;
All honoured, all revered, has come,
With hoary head, unconquered home ;

Home to his recompense above,
Enshrined in prayer, entombed in love,
At last the Hero, bowed with years,
Yet stout of heart and free from fears

(The good can know no fears), in death
Has bent his brow, has given his breath ;
And all the nation, sorrowing,
Laments its Councillor and King.

The last sad fight so brief ! Oh, say,
That Death victorious feared to stay,
Lest he, unbeaten in the strife,
Should win the victory of life.

A victory he truly won,
Britannia's best and bravest son ;
For now in death the warrior lives
That life of peace which Jesus gives.

POETIC IMMORTALITY

THERE is no limit to the glorious strife
    Of human intellect that men call Life.
Some wither in their youth ; some in their prime
Yield to the chances, not the lapse, of time.
Some in old age, like stately trees, prepare
With dauntless heart the common fate to share.
Yet all alike, for they who fall in youth
But teach mankind this everlasting truth,
That Poets never die, but live sublime
In the sweet measure of their deathless rhyme.

CHILDHOOD

THE tear in childhood's eye
 Is like the morning dew ;
The sunlight of their sky
 Beams ever fresh and new,
And seems to have a fairy pow'r
To dry the raindrop of an hour.

The smile in childhood's cheek
 Is like the blush of morn,
When many a rosy streak
 Tinges the yellow corn,
And brightens every feature's mould,
And turns the landscape into gold.

The frown on childhood's brow
 Is like an autumn day,
When the first flakes of snow
 In a moment melt away.

Oh ! happy age that ever wears
At the same instant smiles and tears !

Too soon, 'tis hard to dry
   The tear, or teach to smile—
The one, hypocrisy,
   The other, worldly guile ;
For manhood's passions ever blight
Our childhood's rose that bloomed so bright !

THOUGHTS ON FLOWERS

THERE are thoughts like violets, hidden
    'Neath foliage dark and thick ;
There are thoughts that rush unbidden,
    And make the dull heart beat quick.

There are thoughts like sunflowers, courting
    Every wanton amorous ray ;
There are thoughts ill bear consorting
    With the pure warm breath of day.

There are thoughts like summer roses,
    Shedding fragrance all around ;
There are thoughts no man discloses,
    Thoughts to night and silence bound.

There are thoughts like myrtles, lending
    Bright grace to festal hours ;
There are thoughts that, gaily blending,
    Shine as coronals of flowers.

There are thoughts like lilies, peerless
　　In their white and chaste array ;
There are thoughts so firm and fearless,
　　Death for them has no dismay.

There are thoughts like cedars raising
　　Their vast gnarled hands above ;
Thoughts of prayer, and faith, and praising ;
　　Thoughts of peace, and hope, and love.

THE SILVER-WINGED DOVE

ROUND the porch of my cottage convolvulus twines
  With woodbine and ivy, a garland of spring;
And a low-browed straw thatch with broad corners declines,
  And tempts the young swallows so nimble of wing.

An old oaken settle, placed somewhat aslant
  To catch the late sunbeam, yet shield from the glare
Of the hot noon-tide rays, which make all nature pant,
  Draws an idler like me from his dinner's plain fare.

Fresh roots from the garden, a chick from the yard,
  With a rasher fresh cured from my own little farm,
And a glass of home-brewed that no foe could call hard—
  Such my banquet ; I like it, and where is the harm ?

No woman to plague me, or love me—the same—
  For kissing and scolding seem often a pair
Of benefits given the married to tame,
  Or troubles allotted the single to scare.

So I sit on my settle, my pipe in my mouth,
    And banish such follies, such troubles, as love ;
But above in her cage there hangs straight to the south
    One who coos in all weathers, my silver-winged Dove.

A SOCIETY LYRIC

INTO the shadow, into the shade
  Where lives are forgotten and surely fade
    In the midst of a slow decay;
What if there rises a kindly sigh,
Or a tear for the past lurks still in the eye?
    No matter—he's had his day.

Into the shadow, into the shade,
Where many a broken heart is laid,
    And the feet that wandered away
Pace painfully back to the early light
Of hours once hopeful, pure and bright.
    No matter—she's had her day !

Into the shadow, into the shade,
Where a cold retreat from care is made
    And lips refuse to pray;

Where vain regret and the foolish vow
Sadden the heart and wrinkle the brow.
  No matter—they've had their day!

Out of the shadow, out of the shade,
By the gracious promise God has made,
- Our sins and our sorrows past,
Into the sunshine, into the light,
Cheered by His mercy and strong in His might—
  This matters, and this will last.

TO A BEAUTIFUL YOUNG LADY

OH ! why wilt thou sully thy beauty, my dear,
  With the pigments and dyes that a courtesan uses,
When Nature has made thee without a compeer
And Liberty gives thee the love that she chooses ?

Oh ! fly from the peril that grows in the touch,
Till Roses and Lilies have nothing to offer,
And the Peony flaunts on thy cheek over-much,
And thy loveliness falls a sad prey to the scoffer.

OLIVER MONTAGU'S DOG 'BOXER'

SHOT BY A KEEPER IN WINDSOR PARK, AFTER FOLLOWING HIS
MASTER THROUGH THE EGYPTIAN CAMPAIGN

BURIED AT MARLBOROUGH HOUSE, JUNE 1883

HERE, scarce a league from Paul's historic Dome,
    Where the tall elm trees shade a Royal home,
Lies a true Friend! For man or dog what name
Can more ennoble or enhance his fame?
O'er the parched desert, through the midnight fray,
Where his fond master led the glorious way,
He bravely followed, and with mute caress
Cheered both his labour and his idleness.
A miscreant slew him! None was near to save.
Let honest tears bedew his honoured grave,
And willing hands entwine his funeral wreath—
A trusty comrade is at rest beneath!

LINES

ADDRESSED TO MR. MATTHEW DAWSON

BY 'ONE OF THE STABLE,'

WITH A BOOK OF SONNETS BY THE SAME AUTHOR

Better to be the Prince of Trainers,
Than the Trainer of Princes.
Proverbs (Revised Edition).

'TIS thine, great Matthew, by the laws of fate
    To train the young and teach them to run straight.

So may it be the duty of my muse

To seek the good, the worthless to refuse ;

To guide the footsteps of reluctant youth

And keep them straight upon the path of Truth :

To press them here, and there, perchance, restrain ;

Now use the spur and now the tightened rein,

Yet save my greatest efforts for the close,

And win the race—if only by a nose.—

Thus may our mutual labours bring success,

And make our own and others' happiness ;—

Though still the advantage must with thee.remain---

Thou hast the nobler animal to train !

NEWMARKET : *July* 1, 1884.

LINES TO 'FLY'

A FAVOURITE TERRIER BORN IN INDIA,

AND KILLED BY FALLING THROUGH THE ROOF OF A HOUSE

WRITTEN FOR LADY EBRINGTON

FROM Eastern climes an English heart she brought
    (For Love a teacher is, herself untaught).
Her little life was loving and beloved,
Her little weaknesses were when she roved.
For nature never changes; you may scan
The self-same freaks in terrier or in man.
Alas! our weaknesses are strong! at length
Poor Fly was victim to their very strength!
Unlike her namesake that the window treads,
And safely walks the ceiling o'er our heads,
She, eager for the chase and overbold,
Lost in a moment her firm footing's hold,
And, toppling from the giddy roof, she fell
A mangled corpse—this dog we loved so well!

U

My heart is sore, and still my Mother weeps ;
For where is love if honest sorrow sleeps?
The world may find me many another friend,
But none more true—may none so sadly end !

December 3, 1887.

GLENQUOICH

GLENQUOICH ! here may misanthropes recall
   The first fond visions of their infancy,
Ere yet their early sweetness turned to gall,
And the fresh fountain of their hearts ran dry.
Here may the woe-worn wretch forget his grief,
And smile with new-found pleasure once again—
Here in thy heathery wilds find sure relief,
And live oblivious of his former pain ;
For Nature here, with outstretched arms, invites
Each passer-by to share her glad delights,
Not rugged wild, to bruise with stern caress,
But blent with art, a cultured wilderness
Far from the abodes of man, yet all unite,
With one accord—the young, the fair, the bright
To this blest spot to pay their homage come,
And worship Nature in her mountain home.

1855.

THE FEAST OF BELSHAZZAR

I T is the night when in the vaulted hall
   The King Belshazzar holds high festival;
And where each pillar rears its massive head,
In solemn pride the glittering feast is spread.

Around the throne, where countless gems combine
With every hue to form a scene divine,
Where cup and chalice, 'graved with cunning hand,
Spring from the board as from enchanter's wand;
Where topaz, emerald, diamond, lend a ray
To mock at night, and e'en surpass the day;
A thousand forms in bright array repose,
Their tresses twined with myrtle and with rose,
A thousand lamps, suspended from on high,
Soothe with a softened beam the dazzled eye,
And half reveal the sculptured bowers above,
That woo delights, and breathe the sweets of love.

Lute, timbrel, harp, and many-stringèd lyre
Pour through the aisle harmonious notes of fire ;
A thousand voices, floating softly, give
A deeper charm, and bid the music live ;
While from the board, like sunbeams from a stream,
In lustrous beauty, an unwonted gleam
Of gold and silver flashes in the glare ;—
All hallowed vessels from the House of Pray'r.

How fair the scene !   No brighter here on earth
Could banish care, or give the rein to mirth.
What though the drunkard's heart a moment quail !
What though the sinner's cheek a moment pale !
Away with thought—the flowing wine cup drain ;
Thus drown all care, thus drive away all pain.
But now no thought appals the drunkard's heart,
Remorse may now no single pang impart ;
They fear no wrath ; defying heaven above,
This night they vow to revelry and love.

Oh ! thus, Oh ! ever thus, in pleasure's hour
We scoff at peril, and defy its power ;
Yet when the distant storm at length draws near,
Our hearts o'erwhelmed confess the conscious fear ;

So now Belshazzar in his ' pride of place,'

In pomp exulting, runs his impious race,

Defiant, heedless.   Lo ! the hour is come,

And bowed by fear the tyrant meets his doom.

Oh ! in that awe-struck form the eye might scan

The strength of sin, the nothingness of man.

Why pales the monarch's brow, why turns his eye

As from some spectral form of memory ?

One hand, uplift, with quivering grasp retained

The reeking goblet he but now had drained,

As though unconscious that the life, which shone

In liquid purple o'er its gems, was gone ;

The other rested with a soft caress

On one who vied with light in loveliness,

Whose dark eyes glanced like stars at dewy eve—-

Eyes, whose bright twinkling might the stars deceive ;—

While o'er her beauteous brow, as calm and white

As snow-drifts glistening in the pale moonlight,

A wayward tress escaping from its place

In wild luxuriance, veiled the mute embrace.

Yet e'en that loved one, in her secret breast,

Longs, longs in vain, for virtue's holier rest ;

For Pleasure's flowery path and wanton smile
Again deceive her, and again beguile,
 Lure the fond heart astray, all care remove,
And tangle memory in the toils of love.
As some vast furnace, heaped with glowing fire,
Feeds on itself till every spark expire ;
Till, at the last, of fire, of life, bereft,
A charred and blackened frame alone is left ;
So with man's heart, heaped up with fierce desire,
A very furnace, feeding on its fire,
Awhile the flame may glow ; yet day by day,
More and more dim, it smoulders o'er its prey,
Till but a scorched and withered mass remain,
And for that goodly form we search, but search in vain.

As when a vessel pillowed on the breast
Of southern seas, is softly lulled to rest,
The sail flaps idly to the wanton breeze
That tells of peace, and liberty, and ease ;
The sailors, grouped in many a merry throng,
Pass the gay jest, or sound the careless song,
Till yon small cloud, that slowly wends its way
Unmarked, unheeded, o'er the orb of day,

Uplifts the ocean with terrific force,
And buries all beneath its headlong course,
Strikes the doomed vessel in her peaceful sleep,
And with one swoop engulphs her in the deep:
So with the king, as slowly, yet as sure,
The cloud has burst o'er slumbers as secure;
Unmarked, unseen, it crept along the sky,
And doomed Belshazzar with itself to die .
Now is the time, God's holy house profaned,
Stript of its vessels—what but death remained ?
A human hand, with spectre fingers came,
And wrote upon the wall in words of flame,
' Mene, Mene, Tekel, Upharsin ; ' words
Of unknown import pierced his heart like swords.
No more the circling goblet passes round,
No more the notes of melody resound ;
Rings the light jest no more, no laugh is there :
All, all is hushed, save murmured sounds of prayer.
E'en lips that mocked but now the very name
Strove half in vain a smothered prayer to frame ;
Tore from their dabbled locks the wine-stained flower,
And feebly called on God's Almighty power.

DISCIPLINE

TO conquer hate, to learn the blessed art
    That rules the mind, and teaches to forgive ;
To govern every impulse of the heart,
    And, when one fain would die, to seek to live—

This is a Christian's task—a holy strife—
    Love's purest labour, bringing tenderest gains :
The death of sin that crowns a virtuous life
    Is the rich guerdon Discipline obtains.

AUTUMN

FAST fall the sheaves of heavy corn
    Into the reaper's rugged hand;
    And golden Autumn o'er the land
Pours out the plenty of his horn.

Ah me! in spring how green the shoot,
    In summer-tide how strong and fair;
    What marvel then, if, free from care,
In autumn I should look for fruit?

I look in vain! The seasons roll
    In a doomed cycle—round and round;—
    Sun, Frost, Dew, fertilise the ground;
But barren raindrops flood my soul.

Barren to me, whose soul can ne'er
    A second crop of love bring forth;
    Barren to thee, whose spring-tide worth
Was such as richest autumns bear.

DIMIDIUM ANIMÆ MEÆ

IF half my life with thine be gone,
  And half my soul to realms of shade ;
  And if some converse there be made
Between them, I am not alone :

Each pulse that throbs, a kindred sense
  Awakens in another sphere,
  And, though I cannot clasp thee here,
'Tis something of omnipotence

In spirit-commune to exchange
  Our waking dreams, our dreaming loves
  And still as each emotion moves
To feel that nothing can estrange

The invisible from what I see,
  The infinite from what I hold :
  Oh ! joy of joys in growing old,
For where thou art I soon shall be !

TO THEIR ROYAL HIGHNESSES

THE PRINCE AND PRINCESS OF WALES

ON THEIR SILVER-WEDDING DAY, MARCH 10, 1888

ACCEPT this tribute to fond wedded troth,
  Offered in duteous loyalty to Both!
The perfect love that casteth out all fears
Has blessed your lives for five-and-twenty years,
And hope, in every patriot breast instilled,
Is on this happy day-of-days fulfilled.
A Silver Wedding-day has rarely shone
On nobler duties and more nobly done!
Thy Princess 'Bien-aimée' must always look
Like the good fairy of a story book!
Her youthful mien and regal grace combine,
Like ivy, round the nation's heart to twine;
They smile defiance to the shafts of Time,
The words of envy, or the deeds of crime,

And live in grateful hearts, that welcome here
A Prince and Princess that have no compeer.
Oh, may their ' Silver ' softly change to ' Gold,'
And Love grow fonder as the Loved grow old !

TO LADY AVELAND

DEAR Lady, could there any chance be sweeter
    Than finding, with the magic name of Peter
This little Silver Apostolic Spoon?
A fond renewal of your Honeymoon
That, silvered o'er by five-and-twenty years,
Like a new wedding on this day appears.
God keep it so, in silver chains, yet free,
Lulled by the faithful notes of memory!
Not always Sunshine are the years of love,
But Love makes Sunshine, as this day can prove;
And if a passing shower or chilling wind
Breaks on you—cruel only to be kind—
They show us all how well your heart can bear
Alike the Sunshine and the colder air.
Accept my little gift!   May Peter live
In grace and goodness, and to manhood thrive,
And may we all survive to greet and bless
The Golden Wedding of your happiness!

LOVE THAT LASTS FOR EVER

A JUBILEE LYRIC

1887.

(Published by Command of the Queen)

I

THERE is a Word,
   A Linnet lilting in the grove,
Keen as a sword,
And pure as Angels are above ;
This little Word good men call Love.

II

It bears a Name,
Unsullied by the taint of wealth ;
   Careless of Fame,
And bright with all the hues of health,
It shrinks from praise, to bless by stealth.

III

I join it now
To thine, Victoria !   Thou hast seen
With clear eyes, how
To win it : blessèd hast thou been
With Love, as Mother, Wife, and Queen.

IV

Love bathed in Tears,,
To Love cemented, ever brings
And ever bears
A chastened spirit, that in Kings
Is noblest among earthly things.

V

Come, lasting Love !
For Sweetness in a moment dies,
And all things prove
That Beauty far too quickly flies
From blue, or black, or hazel eyes.

VI

Youth is a snare ;
Like an awakening dream it speeds,
   Nor cries, *Beware !*
A dream of unaccomplished deeds,
A hope of undetermined creeds.

VII

Is it Friendship then ?
The Tyrant of a summer day,
   The boast of men
Who loiter idly on life's way,
A band who neither work nor play.

VIII

Nay ! Friends, though dear,
Pass on their way—change—turn aside ;
   A transient tear
Dims Friendship's light—or some pale bride—
For Love was born when Friendshid died.

IX

Thou, Grey or Gold,
Alone, Great Love, survivest all,
    All else grows old ;
Their birth, their growth, their rise, their fall,
Immortal only at thy call.

X

Love conquers Death
And is Life's portal, and the Soul
    Whose Heavenly breath
Inspires all Life, and ages roll
To ages, and yet leave it whole.

XI

Come then, Great Love,
To whom none ever plead in vain,
    Come from above—
Where are no sighs, no tears, no pain--
And make us pure from selfish stain.

XII

Come, fresh as morn,
When golden sunrise laves the land,
And gilds the corn ;
Come smiling—come with open hand—
That brooks no chain—owns no command.

XIII

Thy voice sounds best
When faint the weary toilers sigh,
And long for rest ;
The tone is clear, but not too high,
With just one touch of mystery.

XIV

Come, calm as night,
When Dian, with her stars, looks on
A wondrous sight—
A sleeping world :—Endymion
Slept thus for thee, pale Amazon !

XV

Be with us now ;
Illume our pleasures, soothe our woes,
        And teach us how
Thy sweet encircling spirit knows
The heart's unrest—the heart's repose.

XVI

Be with us now ;
A Day of many-sided thought
        That curves the brow
With lines of memory, interwrought
With hope, and gratitude unbought.

XVII

Oh Queen ! this Day
Thy people, generous and just,
        As well they may,
Confirm anew their sacred Trust
Enshrined in half a century's dust.

XVIII

For fifty years
Thy people's love has been content
(In spite of tears,
And bitter sorrows sadly blent)
To raise to thee Love's monument.

XIX

A Trophy, based
On duty done, on faction quelled,
No deed defaced
By broken word, or faith withheld,
No foe by stratagem compelled.

XX

Not stone or brass—
These perish with the flight of Time
And quickly pass ;
But Love endures in every clime,
Eternal as the Poet's rhyme.

XXI

Not brass or stone—
These will corrode, and some day die ;—
But Love alone
Laughs at decay, and soars on high—
In fragrant immortality.

XXII

Thy Royal Robe
Is starred by Love : its purple Hem
Surrounds the Globe :
But true Love is the fairest Gem
Of thy Imperial Diadem.

XXIII

Queen of the Sea !
What prouder title dignifies
A Monarchy ?
The Orient owns it, and it lies
Amidst thy countless Colonies ;

XXIV

A wayward realm,
Yet ruled in Love for the world's gain ;
    Thou guid'st the Helm
That brings our commerce o'er the main,
And makes us rich without a stain.

XXV

The Sisters Nine
Were all thy friends ; a willing guest
    Each one was thine,
In turn to cheer, or give thee rest ;
Thy choice, they knew, was always best.

XXVI

And Science came
To meet thee, and enrich thy store
    With Heaven-sent flame,
To burn—like Vesta's lamp—before
A sacred altar as of yore.

XXVII

Thy welcome gave
New impulse to her, and each day,
Like a freed slave,
She worked in Love such deeds, her ray
Shed light and truth around thy way.

XXVIII

No tongue can tell
Thy peaceful triumphs ; mighty War
Has his as well ;
But Peace has greater, nobler far
Than the chained victims of his Car.

XXIX

Thy Jubilee
Is marked by Love ; 'tis all thine own,
And given to thee
By all—a sweet flower fully blown,
The grace and grandeur of thy Throne.

XXX

'Tis thy just meed
For fifty years of righteous reign ;
No heart doth bleed
In all thy kingdom, but the pain
Throbs in thine own, and not in vain.

XXXI

I pray thee take,
In some exchange for all the good
That thou dost make,
The troubles thy brave heart withstood,
Thy temperate yet undaunted mood,

XXXII

These grateful lines ;
As the sweet myrtle wreathes the bay
And intertwines
The classic leaf, e'en so I may
Entwine my chaplet with this Day

XXXIII

'Tis a poor song,
By one whose heart has ever been
Loyal and strong,
And who, like Simeon, now has seen
His hope fulfilled :—GOD SAVE THE QUEEN !

PRINTED BY
SPOTTISWOODE AND CO., NEW-STREET SQUARE
LONDON

www.ingramcontent.com/pod-product-compliance
Lightning Source LLC
Chambersburg PA
CBHW020946030726
47496CB00005B/1378